The Mystery of Castle MacGorilla

The Mystery of CASTLE MacGorilla

By
DAVID BENTLEY HART
and
PATRICK ROBERT HART

Illustrations by
JEROME ATHERHOLT

Angelico Press

First published in the USA
by Angelico Press 2019
Copyright © David Bentley Hart & Patrick Robert Hart 2019
Illustrations copyright © Jerome Atherholt 2019

For information, address:
Angelico Press, Ltd.
169 Monitor St.
Brooklyn, NY 11222
www.angelicopress.com

ISBN 978-1-62138-486-1 pbk
ISBN 978-1-62138-487-8 cloth
ISBN 978-1-62138-488-5 ebook

Book and cover design
by Michael Schrauzer
Cover image: Jerome Atherholt

Humbly — if Impertinently — Dedicated to the Memory of
THE GREAT PETER CECIL BULL (1912–1984),
Thespian, Practical Philosopher, Tireless Advocate
for Teddy Bears Everywhere

Any resemblance between the characters in this book and a collection of soft toys who live in a closet in the Hart household, or a dog generally found lying about somewhere in that same household, is entirely intentional. Permission was obtained from all parties concerned.

CONTENTS

Some time around the middle of the twentieth century, and a little off the beaten path . . .

CHAPTER 1

Arrival at the Castle

THEODORE BEAR—WHO WAS CALLED TEDDY BY HIS friends and who, just by coincidence, happened to be a teddy bear, small and tan and always quite dapper in his neat red bow tie — gazed with quiet excitement through his compartment window as his train pulled into the station at Inverness. He had wanted to visit Scotland for some time, and most particularly this part of the Highlands, so that he could drop in on his old friend Gorilla MacGorilla, with whom he had been in school years before at the prestigious Advanced Academy for Soft Toys in New York City. Until very recently, however, he had been unable to make the journey, because his job as a detective in the stolen goods division of the New York City police department had simply taken up too much of his time.

Now, however, he was free to move about as he liked. A month earlier, after solving the most difficult case of his career (the mystery of the missing tea cozies), he had retired early from the force so that he could pursue a career as a daring international photographer and adventure novelist. No sooner had he collected his final paycheck and bought a new, bright blue camera, than he received an elegant banana-scented invitation to come to Gorilla's ancestral home, Castle MacGorilla, for the grand celebration of Gorilla's elevation to the title of Laird. It was a position that, until recently, had been held by Gorilla's uncle; but the older ape had decided it was time for a permanent change of location and had retired to a family estate on the Isle of Man, relinquishing his title in the process.

The pale gleaming waters of the River Ness and the distant Moray Firth had come into view under an ominously gray late autumn sky, and the train was just drawing to a halt, when the ticket collector — an old man who looked rather like a trout with a large mustache — slid the compartment door open, thrust in his head, and loudly announced, "Inverness! We've arrived at Inverness! Everyone going to Inverness should get off the train here! Reet here!" Then he furrowed his fishy brow. "After all, if ye don't ye'll only be carried on to the next station, and then ye'll only have to buy a ticket back, and that'll be a dark bitter day for everyone, me included, as I'll probably get the blame."

"Oh," said Teddy, quickly gathering up his camera bag and blue suitcase, "yes, of course. I think I'll get off now."

"Aye, ye will," said the ticket collector with a scowl, and then set off down the corridor. A moment later, his voice rang out again, a little farther away: "Inverness! We've arrived at Inverness! Everyone going to Inverness should . . . "

* * *

As Teddy stepped down onto the platform, he found the air considerably colder than he had expected. Overhead, the sky seemed to be growing darker by the moment. All about him, the two dozen or so other passengers who had alighted from the train were hurrying with clear purpose towards their several destinations; only he was standing still. He had been told that someone would be there to meet him, but as yet he could see no sign of a greeting party. After several seconds, however, he did see a tall, thin porter with large spectacles and a rather round nose approaching him. This seemed hopeful.

The porter came to a halt before Teddy and, in a deep and affable voice, said, "Excuse me, sir, but are ye by any chance travelling up country to Castle MacGorilla?"

"Why, yes," Teddy replied.

"Excellent, sir, excellent," said the porter. "I only ask because a canine gentleman from the castle — the chauffeur, I believe — is just inside the station, and he asked me if I would perhaps keep an eye oot for a small soft toy gentleman . . . or perhaps I should say gentlebear . . . and a small lady pig from London, also of the stuffed and fluffy variety."

"A pig?" said Teddy. "Did he say who it was? Did he say . . . ?"

But Teddy's words were cut short by a high, delighted, and slightly snortish squeal coming from behind him: "Oh Teddy! Teddykins! This is absolutely *delish*!"

Teddy turned around, already smiling broadly, as a small pink plush pig in a fetching little emerald-green beret came bouncing along the platform towards him on her two rather dainty hind trotters.

"Oh, Teddy," she cried again, flinging her arms around his neck and giving him a mighty hug, "are you here too? I had no idea. This is totally lollipops — absolutely cream tarts!"

"Yes," said Teddy happily, returning the little pig's hug and then gently disengaging himself from her powerful embrace, "but I didn't know you'd be here either, Pigsy old girl. I didn't see you on the train."

"Well, I was just up in first class, in the front car."

"Of course," said Teddy, "I should have known. You always were a first class sort of sow."

The pig's name was (the "c" pronounced like an "s") Porculina, and she too had been at the Academy with Gorilla and Teddy. Hers was an old and prominent family of toy pigs, with many estates all over the south of England, and she herself was the very successful creator and co-owner of *Fluffed and Painted Inc.*, the world's largest manufacturer of cosmetics for soft toys. At school, she and Teddy had been fastest of friends, but they had not seen much of each other since graduation.

"Well, you look just wonderful," said Teddy, "in the very pink of health, if you don't mind my saying."

"Oh, you too," Porculina squeaked, "and it's so good to hear your voice again. It's . . . it's . . . buttercream icing!"

"Excuse me, miss," the porter interrupted, "but I think I should tell ye that a car is waiting for ye, and the weather looks like it's taking a turn for the worse. D'ye have any baggage? I'd be more than happy to carry it for ye."

"Oh, only a few little things," said Porculina, casually waving a trotter towards the far end of the platform where five large pink steamer trunks were piled together.

The porter blanched.

"Are all of those yours?" Teddy asked in amazement. "What's in them?"

"Oh, just what you'd expect," replied the little pig, "just the indispensables. One for my clothes, one for mystery novels, one for necessities — bibs and bobs and things — and then the other two for snacks."

In a faint, tremulous voice, the porter said, "I'll just go and get some help."

*   *   *

Inside the station, while three gasping porters were loading Porculina's luggage into the back and onto the top of the motor car parked out front, the bear and the pig were met by a medium-sized, shorthaired dog with mottled fur, white with gray speckles and large brown patches (including two that entirely covered his ears and eyes), a salt-and-pepper snout, and a handsome glossy black nose; he was wearing a chauffeur's cap and black gloves. "Miss, sir," he said in a pleasant voice, with the faintest hint of a kindly growl behind his very refined Oxbridge accent, "I'm here to take you to the castle."

Porculina stared at him with a look of delighted surprise. "Why, you're a real flesh-and-blood dog, aren't you?" she exclaimed.

"I have that honor, miss," the dog replied with a ceremonious nod. "I'm Rolandus, butler and chauffeur to the castle, as well as the Laird's valet."

"Goodness," said Teddy, "and how long have you had the job?"

"Ever since they replaced my predecessor in the post, sir," replied Rolandus.

"And how long has that been?"

"Ever since I took the job, sir. In fact," — he stood up rather straight and folded his paws behind his back — "my family has been in service to the clan for generations."

"Well, golly," said Porculina, "think of that. I didn't know there were any flesh-and-blooders at the castle. I mean, Gorilla was always so afraid of getting chewed."

The dog arched an eyebrow. "Not a matter of concern in my case, I'm sure, miss. I trust I'm a passably civilized dog."

"Oh, dear," said Porculina, beginning to blush a somewhat deeper pink, "I didn't mean to suggest otherwise. I didn't offend you, did I? I mean, I think you're just ... just porridge and potatoes!"

The dog now arched both his eyebrows.

"Oh, that's good," said the flustered little pig, "honestly it is. It's ... it's like lime and licorice ... Honestly."

Teddy intervened, clearing his throat rather loudly. "Porculina often uses food imagery as a way of expressing approval, or just plain happiness ... or almost anything else. Sometimes it's a bit exotic, I know, but ... well, it's all quite complimentary."

"Yes, sir," said the dog with a polite smile. "Anyway, all of the stuffed members of the castle staff are a bit too short to reach a steering wheel and the pedals at the same time. Perhaps we should be going, though. The sky looks threatening and it's a long journey."

Rolandus led Porculina and Teddy to the car outside — a large, lovely, old-fashioned silver-gray Rolls Royce, whose hood-ornament was the gold figure of a partially peeled banana — and ushered them into the spacious back seat, where they found several warm woolen blankets waiting for them. As Rolandus got into the front seat, he turned to his two passengers and said, "It's a long drive up to the castle, almost two hours in fact, but there are cabinets behind my seat here with some refreshments — a thermos of hot chocolate, another of hot cider, and some sandwiches."

"Sandwiches?" said Porculina. "How wonderful. Golly. What kind?"

"A variety," Rolandus replied, "all particularly ordered by the Laird. There's banana, honey and banana, chestnuts and banana, and — a special American touch for Mr Bear — peanut butter and banana."

"Oh," said Porculina in an almost dreamy voice, "Gorilla always was such a thoughtful chap." Then, leaning back and sighing contentedly, she added, "Any toffees?"

*　　*　　*

The journey was indeed a long one, but Teddy and Porculina had so much catching up to do that they had no time to get bored, and the sandwiches were delicious (Porculina had five, Teddy one). They also quite enjoyed the landscape through which they travelled as they continued up and up into the hills along the constantly winding road: high treeless craggy green knolls, with occasional juttings of bluish granite, capped by a silvery shimmer of frost, and with lower slopes carpeted in heather, no longer in blossom but stirring beautifully in the breeze. As the car drove on, though, they could not help but notice that the sky continued to darken, and now and then small gusts of glittering snowflakes drifted across the windscreen.

At last the huge and elaborate iron gates of the MacGorilla estate came into view, atop which was set a brightly painted relief of the Mac-Gorilla escutcheon: two red quarters with lions playing bagpipes, two blue quarters with half-peeled bananas, a unicorn to one side, and a monkey to the other, all crowned by a banana tree with great languidly drooping leaves. As the Rolls drove up to the gate, there was a sudden flash of bright blue to the left, as a small, fluffy, electric-blue rabbit with a slightly frantic grin on his face hopped hurriedly out of the gatehouse to let the car in, swinging the two large gates wide open.

"That's Mr Blue Bunny," Rolandus remarked, rolling down his window, "the groundskeeper here. He lives in the guardhouse." Then, turning to the rabbit, he called, "Hello, Blue! Everything all right?"

"Oh, absolutely!" replied the rabbit in a high, clear, carroty voice, skipping towards them eagerly, "Couldn't be better. Everyone's here now. Hoorah, if I may say so." Then, sticking his twitching blue nose in at the window and staring back at Teddy and Porculina over Rolandus's shoulder, he almost shouted, "Welcome to the castle, miss. Welcome, sir. Everything's in readiness. I hope I opened the gates to your satisfaction. If not . . ." — a look of exaggerated worry suddenly appeared on the rabbit's face — "I did, didn't I? Oh, dear!"

"Yes, of course, perfectly," said Teddy. "Thank you."

"Absolutely," said Porculina. "Ta so muchly. Buttered toast, really."

Blue Bunny looked at her quizzically for a moment and then, with an even more excited smile, cried out, "Well, see you soon!" and lurched away happily back to the gatehouse.

"What a nice face he has," said Porculina, as the car continued up the long gravel drive.

"A bit anxious, though," said Teddy reflectively.

"He's a . . . hardworking lad," said Rolandus mildly.

At the end of the drive, the car pulled into the large circular gravel lot in front of the castle, and Teddy and Porculina both drew in their breath when they saw what an imposing edifice it really was. "Well, biscuits," said Porculina, "I always knew Gorilla had an impressive home, but this is something out of a fairy tale."

When Rolandus had opened the back doors of the Rolls for them, they stepped out into the lot and stood looking about them for a while, taking everything in. The castle was an immense granite cliff-face of a house, with turrets and high windows and ramparts and parapets with . . . with . . .

"Oh, what are those crinkly thingies at the top of castles called again?" asked Porculina.

"Crenellations, miss," replied Rolandus.

"That's it," she said, "crinkle-ations. I knew it was something like that. Just like the wavy edges of a pie, but squarish."

On all sides there were marble statues — giraffes, giant centipedes, centaurs, bananas, and the like — and far off to the right were gardens with white gravel paths and topiary figures — knights and damsels, drag-ons, dancing pigs, bananas, and so on — and a large clipped hedge that was surely the outer wall of a topiary maze. Beyond that, in the hazy cleft between two hills, there was the pallid sheen of a small lake. And, at the top of the immense stairs leading up to the castle door, a small, dark brown, amiably plumpish sort of figure stood perfectly motionless. After staring up at it curiously for several moments, Teddy asked, "Is that another statue up there?"

Rolandus turned to look. "In fact, no, sir," the dog replied. "It is the Laird, the very MacGorilla himself."

Almost at once, the round, compact little figure seemed to come to life, jumping up and down on its short stout legs and waving both arms, a red Tam o'Shanter in one hand. "Hullo, you two!" a booming, blessedly familiar voice blared down at them. "At last!" Gorilla put the cap on his head and dashed forward, immediately tripping on the top step and tumbling down to the gravel lot head over heels — amid the soft sound of his plush body striking each step in turn and a succession of small cries of surprise such as "Oh, goodness!" and "Dearie me!" and, at the last, a small, somewhat unexpected "Wheee!" — until he came finally to rest in

8

the gravel, in a sitting position practically at Teddy's feet.

With hardly a pause, however, he leapt back up onto his two stout short legs (only half as long as his arms), straightened his hat, and cried, "Don't worry, I'm fine. All my stuffing's in place." He patted both sides of his nearly spherical little head. "Oh, I'm so glad you're here! How I've been waiting to see you both!" And before either could answer, he hugged them — first Porculina, then Teddy, then both at once — with such force that they could not catch their breath for several seconds afterwards. "Well, come on then, let me show you the old hovel," he said with a delirious grin. "Dinner's in two hours, and you'll just have time to change before meeting all my other guests. Oh, this is splendid! Rolandus will see to your things, won't you, Roly old boy?"

The dog winced slightly at that name, but said only, "I may just need a little help with Miss Porculina's luggage. It's very . . . thorough."

"Right-o," Gorilla answered gleefully. "Come on then, you two," he cried, and led his guests up the great stairs towards the large, dark oak doors of the castle.

*   *   *

Once inside, Teddy and Porculina found themselves in a vast vaulted foyer, full of mirrors, statues, dark ruby tapestries, Chinese and Persian vases, and exquisite marble figurines set upon elegant pedestals. Two immense carpeted staircases rose in broad converging crescents to a large open landing above, from which corridors led away to left and right, while far overhead the ceiling was supported by massive beams of oak. On either side was a large arched entranceway opening upon a sumptuous sitting room. And, in the very middle of the great space, on a high oblong base, stood a large dark green marble statue of a noble looking gorilla in medieval tartans, his left hand held downward and clutching a scroll, his right held up before him, triumphantly holding aloft a large bunch of bananas.

"Luscious crumblies!" said Porculina with a gasp. "Who's he?"

"That," said Gorilla positively glowing with pride, "is my illustrated

9

ancestor, the Grand Gorilla of Mickle Fame, the greatest Laird the Mac-Gorilla clan ever knew, maybe the greatest Scottish toy gorilla of them all, and the founder of our whole banana fortune. He built this castle in the fourteenth century."

"Well," said Teddy, looking around him, "he certainly did a good job of it. But," he added with a thoughtful wrinkling of his brow, "I think you must mean 'illustrious ancestor'."

"It was different in those days, of course," said Gorilla. "That was a long time ago. The castle was more like a big stone box surrounded by a ditch back then. There was a moat and a drawbridge and all of that. But my great-grandfather had it all renovated, so that it could be a proper stately home ... well, with a few dungeons, of course. Now we have everything: electricity and modern plumbing and crayons and bubble bath and downy duvets and bouncy ... or, er, I mean *comfortable* mattresses ... Oh, and a much nicer kitchen, with a much larger pantry. But it was the Grand Gorilla who started it all, back in the days before crayons and bouncy mattresses had even been invented."

"Gosh," said Porculina admiringly; then: "I wonder if I could visit the kitch —..."

But at just that moment there was a loud clatter and a sound of brisk footsteps on the landing above, and the three of them looked up to see a rather handsome ginger-hued soft toy dog with floppy ears and slightly curly fur descending the steps, a heavy and loudly rattling black toolbox in his hand.

"Talking of plumbing, here's the very dog," said Gorilla cheerfully. "This is Mr Woof — or just Woof, since he doesn't like formalities — who's here fixing the plumbing in the bath next to your room, Teddy. He's a grand lad with pipes and electrical things and any sort of machinery."

"Aye, weel, that's dealt with," said Woof with an air of impatience. "The gringe-gobbler had got a bit waffled, and I had to scringenate the whole thing, from frip to flurtle."

"Ah," said Gorilla clapping his hands together, "I thought that might be the problem. Either that or I dropped my toothbrush down the drain. Was it hard work?"

Woof shrugged. "Nay, I canna' say that. But, now that you bring the matter up, I did also find your toothbrush daen the drain, as well as a banana, a pair of scissors, a pocket dictionary, a toy whistle, two rubber ducks, and . . . "

"Oh, well, that's all right," said Gorilla, "as long as everything's fixed now."

"Aye, it'll work reet enough," said the dog with a frown, "but sooner or later it'll need the thrimbalator replaced, and a good scrubbing of the blumbroid squints, or the whole thing'll fall to pieces. Now I know that highborn aristocrats like yourself, whose families have grown rich on the backs of working toys, and who're accustomed t' every privilege, can afford to buy everything new, but it does nae harm to save a penny noo and agin. Ye dinna mind me putting it tha' way, I hope."

"Oh, not at all," said Gorilla, "I quite understand."

Teddy cleared his throat. "You do?" he asked, a little startled. "I mean, it sounded just a bit . . . well, a bit rude to me."

"Oh, normally it would be," said Gorilla, "but Woof doesn't mean a word of it. He's just holding up an old family tradition. You see, he comes from a long line of very distinguished . . . now, what's the word again? Something thingy? Aardvarkists, isn't it?"

"It's 'anarchists,' actually," said Woof with a sigh. "He's reet, ye know," he added, turning to Teddy with a somber expression on his face: "I have nothing but the highest esteem for this fine gentle-ape, who's as generous a toy as there is, but my father and his father would be sorely disappointed if I didn't make an effort."

"Golly," said Porculina, "just what *is* an . . . what was it? Ant-artist?"

"Anarchist, ma'am. It's someone who doesna care for laws handed down from above or for governments and classes, and thinks no one should really have power over anyone else, and perhaps no one should have fine estates or great wealth when others don't. Again," he said, "I dinna really feel it m'self, not deep daen inside, but I have to do reet by m' ancestors."

"Well, that's nice," the pig replied. "One should always respect one's elders."

"Aye," said the dog with a nod, "there's the sad burden of it."

"Well, never mind," said Gorilla, patting Woof heartily on the shoulder. "Will you stay to dinner, though?"

"Och, weel," said Woof, grimacing slightly, "I'd love t', of course, but I'm not so sure it's quite in keeping with good anarchist principles, y'know. I mean . . ."

"Oh, nonsense!" cried Gorilla. "Aardvarkists have to eat too, I'm sure. And we don't want any of it to go to waste. Oh please, please, please" — the little gorilla's voice became more imploring and he began hopping anxiously from one foot to the other — "it's so jolly when people come to dinner, and the more guests there are the jollier it is."

"*Weeeel* . . . ." Woof scratched behind one ear thoughtfully. "As ye put it that way, there's nothing I hate so much as wastefulness. Oh, all reet then, aye, I'll dine wi' ye, and gratefully."

"Oh, happy day!" cried Gorilla clapping his hands again. "I'll just ask Roly to set another place. And here he is now."

Teddy and Porculina turned about to see Rolandus standing in quiet dignity a few paces away, no longer in his chauffeur's gear, but in his butler's attire instead: a neatly cut tail-coat, a white wing collar, and a black bow tie. "Excuse me, sir, but Miss Porculina's trunks and Mr Bear's bags are all in their rooms now."

"Good," said Gorilla, "then I suppose it's time to show them up."

"I might just mention, sir," the dog added, "that it seems from the weather report on the radio that we may be in for some snow this evening."

"Really?" said Gorilla with a gleam of joy in his eyes. "What did the announcer say?"

"Well, milord, it seems that a storm has risen . . ."

"Oh, no, not like that!" Gorilla suddenly interrupted, in a pleading voice. "Please say it the way the announcer did!"

"I can't possibly, milord . . ."

"Oh, please!" Gorilla turned to Teddy and Porculina with a look of earnest longing on his face. "He does it so very well! Really, he does!"

Rolandus sighed softly, gazed for a moment at Gorilla with an expression of slightly weary resignation, but also perhaps with the faintest hint of an indulgent smile. "Very well, sir. To be precise, he said:" — the dog coughed, straightened his back, and continued in an accent nothing like his own — "Och, *brrrrr*, it's freezin' oot there! And I didna bring m' Wellies wi' me t' the radio station, nor m' jumper neither! Mark m' words, there's a muckle o' snow on th' way."

"Well, that sounds very scientific," said Teddy in a grave tone, nodding his head thoughtfully. "Is it usual this time of year around here?"

"No, not at all," said Gorilla; "we almost never get any snow to speak of. Nowhere in Britain, really. The Golf Steam, I think it is. Oh, this should be delightful, though." He looked as if he could scarcely contain his excitement. "Do you think we might build a snowman?"

"That would be just fabulous," said Porculina.

"Miss, sir, I had best just show you to your rooms now," said Rolandus. "I'm afraid we're a bit understaffed for dinner tonight, and I should get down to the kitchen to lend a hand."

"Yes, that's my fault," said Gorilla, shaking his head. "We have a bit of a skeleton crew just now."

"Skeletons?" gasped Porculina with a look of alarm in her eyes. "Crumpets!"

"No, I mean we're working with the bare minimum of staff at the moment."

"We frequently are," Rolandus remarked drily.

"Normally, you see," Gorilla continued, "we have ever so many maids working here. I'm not exactly sure how many exactly, but dozens and dozens, I'd guess. How many would you say there are precisely, Roly?"

"Three, sir," replied the dog.

"Yes," Gorilla said, nodding sagely, "that sounds right. Some large number like that. But, anyway, I sent almost all of them away on holiday when I learned that one of them — Lillian, I think — had an aunt who was having a birthday. I thought they should celebrate, and I quite forgot about my own party. I'm a bit forgetful now and then, as you know. And we normally have scores of footmen too, don't we, Roly? How many of those would you say there are?"

"Two, sir."

"Yes, that sounds right. Well, anyway, I sent them away on holiday too. It wouldn't have seemed fair if I had let the maids go but not them. But we'll pull through — even if I have to pitch in myself. I've done it in the past."

A worried expression suddenly appeared on Rolandus's face. "Really, sir, that shouldn't be necessary; I'm sure we'll make do. We anticipate no difficulties, honestly." Then, composing himself and adjusting his tie, he turned to Teddy and Porculina and said, "If you will only follow me, miss and sir, I'll just show you to your rooms." And, gracefully turning on his heels, he led them towards the stairs.

CHAPTER 2

A Grand Banquet

THEY STOPPED FIRST AT PORCULINA'S ROOM. TEDDY had seen such opulent interiors only on a few fleeting occasions in the past, when he had investigated robberies at the homes of the very wealthy, and even those had not boasted so much in the way of rarities and curios. Even Porculina, who was far more accustomed to the life of luxury than he, was a little taken aback by the sheer grandeur of her room's appointments: the immense canopied bed with the elaborately carved posts, the silk wallpaper patterned with fruits and flowers so art-fully rendered that one could almost taste and smell them, the gorgeous antique furnishings, the marble statuettes, the huge mirror in its scrolled gold frame, the Chinese vases full of fresh roses, the mahogany bookcases, the large fireplace with its black marble mantelpiece, the silk-upholstered love-seats, and all the rest. "Blackberry pie and clotted cream!" she said. "It's like a setting for one of my mystery books."

As they entered the room, a pretty soft toy panda in a maid's uni-form and a red woolen scarf emerged from behind the open doors of the wardrobe. "I'm just finishing hanging up your things, miss," she said in a rather sweet voice, "and I've laid out your bibs and bobs at the dressing table and . . . well, in heaps all around it, if you don't mind, miss. I'm not sure I can get to the books and snacks before I have to go down to the kitchen . . . "

"Oh, please don't bother about that," said the little pig cheerfully. "I like looking after all that myself. Really, I'm awfully grateful to you for getting the clothes sorted out so nicely. Really, creamy crunchy thanks."

"This is Panda," Rolandus said, "the only one of our maids who's not away just now. She and her little son Pandulus — handsome little fel-low — are also assistants to the chef, who happens to be her brother-in-law."

"Oh, gosh, an assistant chef. Really?" Porculina was clearly impressed by this. "I've always wanted to do something exciting like that, but I've never been able to cook something without immediately eating it, so, well . . . " She shrugged.

"Yes, miss," said Panda, "I suppose it is exciting in its way, but Pan-dus — that's our chef — he's the real artist. Everything he makes is won-derful — too good to eat, really."

Porculina pursed her lips thoughtfully and slowly shook her head. "I've never really understood that expression," she said.

Teddy nodded. "It is a strange one, isn't it?" he said.

*　　*　　*

After a quick but soothing bath, Teddy dressed for dinner in his room, which was every bit as comfortable — if not quite as lavish — as Porculina's. He donned the dinner jacket he had bought before leaving New York and exchanged his red tie for a black one. As he took a final look at himself in the mirror to make sure everything was just right, he noticed the reflection over his shoulder of a large familiar photograph, hanging on the wall and set in a gilt frame. He turned, walked over to it, and stared at it happily for several seconds. It was a picture of the three of them — Teddy, Porculina, and Gorilla — as they had been in their last year in school together. They were all wearing their purple Academy blazers, and Porculina had a large purple ribbon on her head; they had their arms draped over one another's shoulders and above them, written directly on the picture by Gorilla in bright orange crayon, were the words "Fluffy Friends Forever!"

"Sentimental old simian," Teddy murmured to himself with a smile. Then, in a happy state of mind, he left his room and descended to dinner.

*   *   *

The dining room, which was a converted medieval banqueting hall, was enormous. It had a high ceiling supported by gigantic wooden beams, its walls were draped with rich brocades — scenes of gorillas joyously dancing around maypoles, unicorns dashing through banana groves, winged fairy frogs, badger minstrels strumming their lutes, and so on — and at its far end there was a huge oil portrait of the Grand Gorilla of Mickle Fame sitting upon an elegant rocking horse and eating a banana. The long dining table in the center of the room was of more recent design, set upon a golden carpet like a glowing island in the hall's immensity, covered from end to end by a bright white tablecloth, and illuminated by tall candles burning in silver candleholders.

When Teddy entered the room, all the other guests were already seated.

"Ah, there you are," cried Gorilla from the head of the table, standing up in his ornate high-backed chair. "I was wondering when you'd arrive. Your place is right up here next to me, across from Piggles."

"Oh, dear," said Teddy, hurrying along the length of the table to the chair that Rolandus was holding out for him, "I must be late."

"No," said Gorilla, sitting down again as Teddy took his place, "the rest of us all came early. It's all so exciting, you see."

Teddy looked around at the assembled party. It was an impressive sight. Gorilla was in his best dinner jacket and formal kilt, and Porculina was radiant in a flouncy, pale pink gown that floated about her like a misty gossamer. Blue Bunny was there, wearing a yellow bowtie with green polka dots, all quite striking against the shrill azure of his fur, and Woof was there as well, wearing a dinner jacket and tie that he had obviously borrowed from Gorilla and that did not fit him particularly well (since he was taller than Gorilla but not nearly as round). Then there were a number of other soft toys whom Teddy had not yet met: two frogs, one fully grown and the other not much bigger than a tadpole, each wearing a dark green dinner suit over his bright green skin; an extremely pretty lady Raccoon in a black and white striped ball gown, who looked very familiar in the flickering candlelight (though Teddy was sure he must be mistaken); a gaudy scarlet, blue, and yellow parrot with a violet bowtie about his neck; and, perhaps most remarkable of all, a speckled orange and cream-yellow squid in a sea-green waistcoat and jacket, his head and tentacles half flopping across his place at the table.

"Well, we've all already made one another's acquaintance," said Gorilla to Teddy, "and I've just been telling them all about you. So let me just make a few quick introductions while Rolandus and Panda bring the soup. These two green gentleman"—he indicated the frogs—"are my very dear friends the MacAmphibians, Ribbit and his nephew, whose name I forget, but we all just call him Jumping Bean anyway."

"Actually that is my name," the little frog piped up.

"Oh, there's a happy coincidence, then," said Gorilla. "Anyway, Mr MacAmphibian runs a pest control service—dealing in flies and other bugs—and his nephew there is his apprentice. It's a thriving business too, from what I hear. That's true, isn't it?" he asked, turning to Ribbit.

"Oh, aye, I suppose," said the frog in a croaking voice. "Nain too bad, really. I take in between four and five pence a week, and we get all the flies we can eat, o' course."

"Oh, how scrumptious!" Porculina immediately exclaimed, but then fell silent with a look of uncertainty on her face. "Well . . . maybe not, really. Sorry. Force of habit."

Teddy placed a paw in front of his mouth and pretended to cough. Porculina merely shrugged.

"Nay, but they *are* scrumptious," insisted Ribbit, "if ye only gi' 'em a chance."

"Now, let's see," continued Gorilla, "you've met Woof. And Blue there?"

"We met at the gate," said Teddy. "Hello again, Mr Bunny."

"Just call me Blue," the rabbit called out in a high, almost frantically friendly voice, "please, sir, please. Oh, please."

"Well, please just call me Teddy, then."

"Right-o, will do, sir, most certainly!" Blue Bunny's nose twitched furiously, and his head bobbed up and down so energetically that his long ears looked as if they just might fly off. "I mean Teddy, sir. Oh, dear . . ." — and he began to quiver a little and lowered his eyes.

"And — oh," said Gorilla, "you must know your fellow American, Miss Raccoon — or Miss Raquel de Raccooning, to use her professional name."

"Oh, my goodness!" gasped Teddy with widening eyes, "of course. Why, Miss de Raccooning . . . but you're my favorite film actress. I couldn't be sure it was you in this light, but . . . Why, you're even more beautiful in person . . . if . . . if" — he swallowed — "if you don't mind me saying so."

The lovely Raccoon batted her long lashes and then demurely turned her eyes down towards the table. "Really," she said, in her famously silky voice, "you're much too kind. I'll bet you say that to all the celebrated, award-winning, gorgeous movie starlets you meet."

"Well," said Teddy, sounding a little muddled, "no, I wouldn't say . . . I can't really . . . not at all. You see, honestly, I haven't actually met any others. But even if I had you'd still be my favorite. I've been waiting for your next film for . . ." He hesitated for few seconds. Then, more quietly, he said, "Well, it's been a while now, I suppose."

The Raccoon smiled at him disarmingly, her eyes positively twinkling. "How sweet. Yes, I've been resting. It gets so tiresome, all the filming and the travel and talking to the press and being photographed. And my fans make such demands on my time. I've run away for a little while, you might say." Then, with an even more radiant smile, she added, "Oh, but please — *please* — call me Raquel."

Just then, Rolandus entered the hall with a large covered porcelain soup tureen, which he placed upon a marble-topped sideboard where bowls were stacked, not far from the head of the table. Panda was with him, wearing a fresh starched pinafore and maid's cap, and carrying a large silver pitcher. As the conversation continued at the table, bowls of a pale yellowish soup, from which a deliciously fruity and spicy fragrance rose up, appeared before each guest, and every glass was filled with purple grape juice.

"Quick," said Gorilla, "we have to finish the introductions so we can eat. This" — he indicated the parrot — "is Mr Alasdair MacAw, a very distinguished painter and art critic, from a very accomplished scholarly family of Hebridean toy parrots. I don't know what most of that means," Gorilla added with a slight frown, "but he's made some very pretty pictures if you ask me. Lots of bright colors, and all sorts of interesting things in them, like Merry-Go-Rounds and . . . well, more Merry-Go-Rounds."

"Carousels *are* one of my specialties," said the parrot in a rich and cultured squawk, "but I'm also the curator of a small and, I like to think, distinguished museum of Scottish art and historical relics down in Inverness. Anyway, pleased to meet you, Mr Bear."

"Teddy, please," said Teddy.

"Of course," said the parrot with a gracious dip of his beak, "and please don't hesitate to call me Mr MacAw."

"Ah," said Teddy, a little taken aback, "all right."

"That," said the parrot after a tense moment, "was a joke. I'm not very good at them, I'm afraid. Parrots aren't as a rule. Please, call me

Alasdair, or even" — he opened his beak wide, tossed back his head, and uttered a long, loud, piercing, resounding cry — "AlasdairAwwwwkMac-AwwwwkMacAlasdairAwwwwwwwwwkadairMacAwwwwkkk!" He lowered his head again and politely cleared his throat. "That's what my family and oldest friends call me, at any rate."

As the last of the echoes melted away in the air above, a little flurry of applause passed around the table. Teddy noticed Rolandus, still standing beside the soup tureen, cautiously removing his paws from his ears.

"Golly!" said Porculina, "Buttered scones, but that was impressive! Is that what your mum calls you?"

"Every day," said Mr MacAw, "especially when trying to get my attention."

"Oh, what is this utterly gorgeous smelling . . . ?" Porculina began to ask, turning her attention to her soup.

But Gorilla was already eagerly introducing his final guest. "And this spectacular squid is none other than Mr Conall MacCuttles — or just Cuttles, as he likes to be called. Like many famous folk, he goes by just one name. Maybe you've heard of him — the playwright and poet. He's pretty famous over here at least. At least, so he tells me."

Teddy observed Rolandus in the distance by the sideboard, quietly rolling his eyes. "I'm ashamed to say I haven't," said the bear with an abashed shrug, "but as a policeman I didn't have time to do all the reading I would have liked. I do love poetry and drama, though. What sort of plays and poems do you write, Mr Cuttles?"

The squid limply lifted his head an inch or so, gazed for a moment at Teddy from his large golden eyes, and then said, in a low, gloomy, slightly soggy voice, "Sad ones. Very sad. My poems are . . ." — he took a deep breath, which had something of a bubbly sound to it — " . . . sad . . . and a little wet. And my plays I would call . . . tragical."

"Really?" said Teddy.

"Yes, they're very sad," Gorilla remarked. "Some of them have almost made me cry."

The squid sighed deeply and, in a rather floppy way, nodded morosely. "I'm sad by nature, you see. I think it's because I find writing such a sad business."

"Do you?" asked Porculina. "Why do you do it then?"

"I had no choice, really." Cuttles shook his head and sighed yet again. "You see, I was born with an inexhaustible supply of ink. I had to do something with it. You can't just let ink sit around, you know. It gets . . . sticky . . . and uncomfortable."

"Oh," said the little pig with a sympathetic frown.

"Well," Teddy said, trying to think of a polite question, "is everything you write sad?"

"Yes," Gorilla suddenly interjected, "terribly, terribly, horridly, horridly sad! Why the play he's just written — well, I couldn't get to the end of it, and had to ask Rolandus to stop reading it to me and to put out the light by my bed."

"What's it about, then?" asked Teddy.

Cuttles stared at him ominously. "Are you sure you wish to know? It is not a . . . happy theme."

"Yes . . . I think so."

"Very well," replied the squid a little hesitantly, "if that is what you really want. It is a play about an oyster, a young oyster, full of hope and promise and an innocent confidence in the goodness of life, who . . ." — Cuttles paused for a moment, and his expression grew even more sorrowful — " . . . who loses his favorite red rubber ball. And though he searches for it throughout the play, all forty-two acts, he cannot find it again." The squid's head dropped again, and it seemed as if a tear glittered in one of his entrancingly large eyes.

"That *is* sad," said Porculina with real feeling, and everyone else around the table concurred with nods and murmurs. "But maybe," she added after a few moments, "just maybe he finds it again later, after the play ends."

"That I cannot say," the squid replied. "All I know is that, at the play's end, the ball is still gone . . . quite gone."

For several moments, no one said anything; the mood around the table had become distinctly somber. Then, all at once, Gorilla's expression brightened, and in a merry voice he said, "Well, we've plenty of rubber balls around here, and you can always send that little oyster chap around any time and I'll fix him up with a dozen of them. Anyway, now that the introductions are done, let's eat."

"Oh, yes," said Porculina rapturously, "that reminds me. What is this utterly gorgeous smelling soup? I don't recognize it at all."

"Banana, nutmeg, and saffron," said Gorilla, "one of chef's specialties. Please, try it for all of us and tell us what you think."

Porculina looked around the table, an almost angelic smile on her face, and said, in a modest voice, "Well, I'd love to do the honors." Then, with a last pretty flit of her eye-lashes, she lunged forward, thrusting her snout into the soup and, with a series of loud snorting and grunting noises, devoured it completely in a matter of seconds. Then she raised her face from the bowl — which she had licked entirely clean — daintily dabbed her lips with her napkin and looked about her with an expression of luminous contentment. "Luscious," she said softly, as if deeply moved, "exquisite . . . so banana-ish and nut-meggy and saffrony . . . It's so very, very . . . *tasty*."

*   *   *

The dinner was delightful and everyone seemed to be having a good time — except for Cuttles, who accompanied his meal with soft mournful sighs uttered at regular intervals and occasionally emitted a faint spray of black ink that left small stains on the tablecloth in front of him. After the soup was cleared away, the mixed popcorn course arrived — plain, buttered, and glazed in banana and caramel sauce — along with glasses of fresh coconut milk. Gorilla stared a little enviously at the two frogs, who ate their popcorn with the aid of their long darting tongues, rapidly plucking one kernel after another from their dishes. He even attempted to imitate them, but as his blunt pink tongue reached less than an inch from his lips he was obliged to lean closer and closer to the table as he did so, until he suddenly tipped headfirst into his plate and scattered popcorn everywhere. "Oh, well," he said as he clambered back into his chair, brushing popcorn from his head, "that's such a jolly trick. I wish I could do it."

"Aye, weel," said Ribbit, "ye simply haven't the tongue fer it. Yours lacks the necessary elasticity."

"And stickiness," added Jumping Bean. "It has to be sticky."

Next, to clear the palate, came a bonbon course with chocolate-covered almonds on the side, all of it washed down with banana milkshakes.

"What a marvelous chef you have here," Miss Raccoon remarked when she had eaten her last bonbon. "Wherever did you find him?"

"Just lying about," said Gorilla. "He's been here as long as I remember. He trained in China, of course, as well as Paris and Detroit — he's a very sophisticated chef, really — and I think he'd like to start a restaurant of his own someday. But for now he's all ours."

"Detroit . . . ?" muttered Teddy quizzically.

"Aye, the food's as fine as I've had in a lang, lang time," Woof interjected, "but I have to say I'm not sure I feel quite reet aboot being served at table like this. I'm not sure it's quite in keepin' wi' good anarchist principles."

"Oh, don't bother about that," said Gorilla with a wave of his hand. "I don't like all this formality myself. In fact, I used to try to even things out by occasionally getting all the staff to sit here at table and to let me prepare the dinner and serve it to them. I had a wonderful time doing it, too, and I almost never spilled soup on anyone's head, at least not more

24

than once or twice a meal, and any damage I did to the kitchen I had fixed right away. It was all great fun."

"Was?" said Porculina. "Have you stopped doing it?"

"Yes, well," said Gorilla with a look of perplexity crossing his face, "for some reason they all begged me to. I don't know why." He looked extremely thoughtful for several moments. "I suppose they all missed Pandus's cooking."

"I can see why," Teddy remarked. "One doesn't get cooking like this just anywhere."

"You should taste his ginger-banana biscuits," said Gorilla, "or cookies, as you Americans would say. They just melt in your mouth."

"Ohhh," said Porculina softly, "do they really?"

"Still," Woof persisted, "I dinna know if I feel quite reet. The setting here — weel, it's so grand, isn't it?"

"Yes, I suppose it is," said Gorilla, looking about the hall happily. "The house that bananas built, my uncle likes to call it."

"I've been wanting to ask you," said Mr MacAw suddenly, "why exactly did your uncle step down as Laird?"

"I'm not entirely sure," said Gorilla, "but I expect he was tired of all of the responsibilities that go with the position."

Rolandus, who was just then clearing away plates from the opposite end of the table, turned away suddenly and made a sound like labored coughing, loudly and repeatedly, and only succeeded in containing it after several seconds. When at last he turned around again, he patted his chest and said, "Excuse me, sir, I have a bit of a — a bit of a tickle in the back of the throat."

"You should watch that," Gorilla replied with a look of earnest concern on his face. "One can get quite a chest cold this time of year."

"Thank you, sir," the dog replied, "I shall take every precaution."

"I've been meaning to ask something as well," said Miss Raccoon. "This may sound silly of me, but I've always thought that bananas came from the tropics."

"Yes indeed," answered Gorilla.

"Well, aren't we a bit far north here, then? I mean, I've heard that your family's farms are here in the highlands and on the Isle of Man. Isn't it a bit cold for bananas?"

"Oh, that's all right," said Gorilla. "You see, most of the bananas we grow are used in ice-creams and custards and so forth, so it's all right if they're cold."

"Oh," said the raccoon with a nod, "I see. That makes sense."

Everyone around the table nodded in agreement.

"Ice-cream always depresses me," remarked Cuttles; then, after a moment: "Custard's all right, though — if one likes that sort of thing. For myself, it reminds me too much of ice-cream . . . which I find depressing."

*　　*　　*

The main dish was a richly seasoned banana and plantain casserole, accompanied by caramelized vegetables and glasses of milk. "I like plantains," said Gorilla as it was being served. "They're like bananas but not *too* like bananas, so they set off the flavor of the bananas without clashing with them, if you see what I mean." Everyone at the table pronounced it a very excellent dish indeed, and the conversation flowed happily on, from one topic to another, only occasionally slowed down by some melancholy observation or other on the part of Cuttles. Three more courses passed equally pleasantly — mushrooms on toast, banana sorbet, and oat and banana cakes — and then dessert arrived, in the form of a crème brûlée made from banana custard. This last was so delicious that Porculina actually gave a shrill cry of delight at her first taste of it. Cuttles remarked again that custards made him think of ice-cream, and that ice-cream depressed him, but this did not seem to affect his appetite; only Porculina finished eating before he did.

Afterward, as Rolandus and Panda were serving hot chocolate or hot cider to the guests (Porculina took a cup of each), Miss Raccoon looked down along the table towards Gorilla and, with a radiant smile, said,

"Now, I wonder if our host might tell us a little more about the mysterious history of this castle. I mean, I've heard that there's something of a legend attached to the place. Something about" — she looked around the table with a slightly conspiratorial expression in her eyes — "a treasure with a curse on it."

"Oh, that!" said Gorilla cheerfully. "Yes, that's true."

"There's certainly a treasure," interjected Mr MacAw. "I tried on several occasions to get the previous Laird to donate it to my museum, just for security's sake if nothing else. It's full of precious artifacts from centuries of Scottish history. But I could never convince him. He said he used to play with the treasure as a child and couldn't bear to part with it."

"Yes, it is a jolly sort of treasure," said Gorilla, "except for the curse. It's a very big treasure, made up of all the little treasures that my illustrated ancestors collected over the generations."

"I think you mean . . ." Teddy began to say.

"There's gold and there are jewels," Gorilla continued, "and paintings by the great toy gorilla masters of the past, in oils and finger-paints, and crowns and scepters from the royal treasure hoards of ancient toy gorilla kings and queens, and so on and so forth. And I've added some pieces of my own — some especially nice rubber balls and a beautiful paperclip necklace. And, well, we keep it all down the hallway somewhere, over in that direction, or . . ." He seemed not to know precisely where he was pointing; his hand floated before him inconclusively, drifting now one way and now another, until he finally gave up and set it down, not seeming to notice that he had placed it in his custard. "Well, somewhere around. Rolandus could tell you. Would you like to see it?"

"Oh, yes," said Miss Raccoon enthusiastically, "if we can."

"But what about the curse?" asked Jumping Bean. "It sounds dangerous."

"Not to worry," said Gorilla. "That only applies to anyone who might try to steal the treasure — which would be very rude, if you ask me."

"Aye, but is it really a curse, though?" asked Woof. "I mean, tha's all nae more than a legend, surely."

"No, there's a curse all right," said Gorilla, his voice becoming all at once a little somber, "and not one to be trifled with. It all goes back to my ancestor Angus MacGorilla, the fourth Laird of the Castle. He was a very strange sort of Highland toy gorilla. He dabbled in magic, you see. Originally his only hobbies were boating and rocking-horsing, but he kept getting them confused and trying to cross the loch on a rocking-horse, so he gave up on boating altogether and devoted himself to magic lore — the casting of spells, the making of potions, pulling rabbits out of bonnets, that sort of thing. Well, when he was Laird, he began to fear that the castle might be besieged and the treasure carried off — Scotland was a lawless land in those dark days — so he cast a spell over the treasure, one that would bring misfortune to any thief who dared to steal it, and then let the curse be known far and wide." Gorilla's voice grew quieter now and a look of deep seriousness came over his features. "And a terrible, dreadful, dire curse it was. I can scarcely bear to think about it."

For several moments no one said anything. The mood in the room had become palpably anxious. At last, with a faint tremor in her voice, Porculina said, "Yes, but what exactly *is* this curse?"

Gorilla shook his head sadly. "Well, since you ask, it states that any-one who is so bold as to lay larcenous paws upon the riches of Castle MacGorilla shall be caught and brought to justice within three days of the theft and then . . . No, no . . . I can't bear to say it." He looked away from the table.

"Please," said Teddy, "we have to know. You've made us too curious."

A murmur of accord fluttered around the table.

Gorilla sighed deeply, shook his head, and then turned his eyes back to his guests. "Very well, then, I suppose I have to tell. The curse goes on to say that, when the miscreant is caught, everyone shall . . . be . . . very . . . very . . ." — Gorilla closed his eyes — "very . . . angry at him."

A collective shudder passed through the room. Porculina gasped. Miss Raccoon looked for a moment as if she might faint. Cuttles groaned deeply, as if in despair. Ribbit hurriedly tried to cover his nephew's ears. Blue

Bunny's teeth chattered audibly and he stared frantically around the table at the other guests. Woof bowed his head in an attitude of emotional defeat. The flames of two of the candles on the table suddenly guttered and went out. No one said a word for nearly a minute.

Then, all at once, Gorilla's face resumed its normal expression of cheer and, in a voice brimming over with merriment, he said, "Well, then, shall we all go and see it now?"

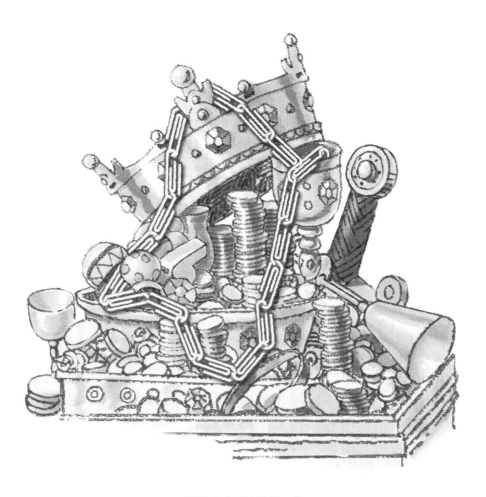

CHAPTER 3

A Robbery in the Night

GORILLA LED HIS GUESTS (WHO WERE WHISPERING among themselves excitedly) down a long, dimly lit corridor, around several bends, up a narrow flight of stairs, across a landing overlooking a large room full of armor, dust, cobwebs, and rubber balls of various sizes, through two large doors with great iron handles, up an even narrower spiral staircase, and finally into what — once Gorilla had switched on the lights — appeared to be a large, bare dormitory from which all the beds had been removed. Everyone looked around in perplexity for some time.

"Umm," Porculina finally said, "not to be a stale biscuit or anything, but I don't actually see any treasure here."

Gorilla's brow furrowed. "Goodness, that's curious," he remarked. "I wonder what's become of it."

Just then the sound of Rolandus clearing his throat came from the doorway and everyone turned around. "Excuse me, sir, not to intrude," said the dog, "but the treasure room is actually at the other end of the castle, not very far from the front door. Blue might have told you . . ."

The rabbit gave a sudden shrill squeal and gazed about with frightened eyes. "Should I have? I didn't think it was my place." He bit his lower lip with his prominent upper incisors and his ears drooped.

"That's all right, Blue," said Rolandus. "It wasn't a criticism. Anyway, ladies and gentletoys, this used to be the junior maids' quarters back in the nineteenth century."

"Oh, that's right!" cried Gorilla happily. "Of course, how silly of me! This is the room where the treasure *isn't*. I always get it confused with the one where the treasure *is*. Well . . ." He grinned and looked around at his guests encouragingly. "Well, off we go then."

The party returned the same way it had just come, this time with Rolandus leading the way. Cuttles brought up the rear, as he could not walk very quickly, and along the way he occasionally murmured, "You needn't worry about me trying to keep up," or "It's not so easy walking, either on one's tip or on one's tentacles," or "If I get lost, the suffering will no doubt be good for me." The others, however, could not hear him over their own animated chatter. When the party reached the dining room again, they proceeded on into an adjacent sitting room, and from there into the main foyer, through the sitting room opposite, and to a green baize door set at its far end. "This, in fact," said the dog with a patient smile, "is the treasure room of Castle MacGorilla."

"Well, you can see how I got confused," said Gorilla. "The other room had a door also."

"Yes," said Teddy, "of course."

Rolandus opened the door, reached in to turn on the lights at the wall switch, and then stepped back. "If you please, ladies and gentletoys."

The guests filed through the door, into a spacious but not enormous room, its dark wooden walls covered with huge paintings of very elegant and obviously aristocratic toy gorillas wearing the varied garbs of earlier centuries. There was one large window with its heavy crimson drapes drawn, and there was a fireplace with a mantelpiece of mottled peach marble, supported at either end by a marble column carved in the figure of a great banana. Atop the mantelpiece stood several ornate Chinese vases, one of which contained some white lilies with long stems. Underfoot was a ruby carpet patterned in gold with images of dragons, seahorses, winged frogs, bananas, and toy whistles. And in the center of the room, on a massive oval pedestal with a multiple terraced top, stood a glorious and gleaming chaos of gold and silver and gems and a few brightly colored rubber balls. Small caskets lay open, full of gold coins and every kind of precious stone. There were two jeweled scepters, piles of gold and silver chains and amulets, innumerable brooches and pins and clasps, as well as two swords whose marvelously elaborate hilts were adorned with emeralds, both sheathed in magnificent scabbards encrusted with rubies. And, in a place of special honor, at the very summit of this shining, shimmering, glimmering hoard, stood a great gold crown covered in diamonds, rubies, and emeralds, and rather clumsily draped with a long necklace of paperclips.

"Meringue and marshmallows!" breathed Porculina. "I've never seen anything like it!"

"Tsk, tsk," Woof muttered, "and tut, tut too, I suppose I should say. The ill-gotten plunder of the ruling class, as my grandfather would put it."

"Oh, I don't know about that," said Gorilla. "I don't think any of them were particularly ill when they got any of this. How would they have been able to carry it? It's so heavy."

"It's absolutely gorgeous," said Miss Raccoon in a hushed voice.

"But very sad, as well," remarked Cuttles somberly. "The heaped up spoils of a long and tragic history of failure, betrayal, conquest, and struggle."

Gorilla pondered this for a moment. "Actually it's a rather jolly history," he said. "There weren't really any betrayals or struggles or anything like

33

that to speak of. Just centuries of good banana crops."

But the squid, who seemed not to have heard Gorilla, was still shaking his head (if it was his head) sadly and averting his great, haunted, golden eyes from the treasure. "I can't bear to think about it," he said.

"Oh come now," said Gorilla, obviously a little shocked, "what's nicer to think about than bananas?"

"I don't think that's what he meant," said Teddy.

"I hope not," said Porculina.

"I know I've said it before," Mr MacAw interjected in his squawkish voice, briefly spreading and shaking his brilliant wings in a glittering fan and then folding them about him again, "but the security arrangements here are simply too lax. One of the very good reasons I often gave your uncle for storing all this in the museum is that here it's hardly protected at all. I know this is a castle, but you don't have soldiers and sentinels, as your ancestors did, and you haven't installed any burglar alarms, and there aren't even any locks on most of the doors. The only lock on the door to this room is a sliding bolt on the inside, and that's no good, unless you intend to lock yourself in with the treasure. I doubt you even remember to lock all the windows on the ground floor at night. There's no watchman on grounds other than Mr Bunny, and he doesn't like to stay up late. A few robbers could spirit it all away in a trice."

"Oh, you worry so," Gorilla replied airily. "Who would want silly old treasure like this? And where would they find a trice to put it in? Think of the bother of carrying it about. I mean, I played with it as a little ape and so I'm attached to it, but otherwise..." He paused, gazing at the glittering hoard, and a look of deep satisfaction spread over his face. "Mind you, that is an excellent paperclip necklace. Did you notice it?"

"Yes, of course," said Porculina, "and it certainly is... lovely. Such craftsmanship! Is it your work?"

Gorilla thrust out his chest and grinned proudly. "Well, I don't like to boast..." He looked about at his guests, as if inviting them to share his delight. "It gives the whole collection a sort of finish, doesn't it? The rest just wouldn't be nearly as nice without it."

"Yes, indeed," said Teddy. Then, nodding his head slowly, he added, "But I have to say that, as a former policebear, I do think Mr MacAw has a good point." He pointed at the curtained window. "This is not a very well protected room. It could happen, you know — someone could break in very late at night. I've investigated many robberies in my time, and just a few precautions could have prevented them."

"Aye," said Woof, "and it would be nae trouble fer me t' install some alarms and put some locks in place."

"Oh, nonsense," laughed Gorilla, "you're fussing over nothing. Again, who would want to go to all that trouble? There are a few fine rubber balls here, of course, and that magnificent paperclip necklace, but the rest is just a load of old, heavy antiques. It's not even in fashion any more. Where could you wear a crown like that in public? You never see them on the audience at the cinema or on the shoppers in a toy store."

"Well, actually," said Teddy, "it's a little more complicated than that. You see, all of this is worth money."

"Oh, I know, but most everything's worth money. But what's money worth, then?"

"Yes," said Teddy, "perhaps, but all of this is worth a *very great deal* of money."

"How much is that?" asked Gorilla.

"How much is what?"

"A *very great deal* of money."

Teddy was momentarily at a loss for words. "Well . . . well . . ." He threw his hands up. "*Quite a lot.*"

"Oh," said Gorilla gravely, "yes. That *is* a good deal."

"High finance confuses me," said Porculina. "Let's talk about something else. Perhaps we should all have a little snack."

"Anyway," said Gorilla, "there's the curse. No one would trifle with that."

"Oh, is there trifle?" Porculina asked eagerly.

"Not everyone believes in curses," said Ribbit.

"Really?" said Gorilla. "Well, I do, and I'm sure that if anyone stole any of this it would be back within three days. Anyway, come on, everybody, let's go back into the sitting room and talk about something jollier. Oh, I know!" he suddenly cried. "I can play the bagpipes for you! I've just learned how this past week! It'll be glorious!"

There was silence. A look of terror seemed to pass through the room in a wave, from face to face. After a moment, Woof leaned close to Teddy and whispered, "Aye, I've heard him practicing a time or twae, and — to tell the truth — I'm naen too anxious to repeat the pleasure."

"Yes," said Teddy, also in a whisper, "I remember him taking up the flute when we were in school. We really couldn't wait for him to put it down again."

"Off we go, then," Gorilla said, urging everyone out with sweeping gestures of his arms, "I'll just send Roly for my bagpipes."

But, just as the guests were moving, oddly slowly, toward the door, Rolandus entered the room. "Excuse me, ladies and gentletoys," he said, holding up both his forepaws, "but I fear I have some inconvenient news to impart. I've just been checking the weather, and it seems that while we've been feasting the snow has been falling. It's a blizzard, in fact, and it seems we're quite snowed in."

"Oh, dear," said Mr MacAw, "that's quite a bother. I wasn't planning to stay for the night and have no things with me."

"Neither were we," remarked Ribbit.

"Nay, nor was I," added Woof.

"I've taken the liberty of arranging rooms to be made up for everyone who was not intending to stay," said Rolandus, "and they should be ready within the hour. We also have a fine supply of nightclothes and other habiliments. I do apologize for the inconvenience, but we shall do everything we can to make you comfortable."

"Oh, this is getting jollier and jollier!" Gorilla exclaimed. "The more the merrier! It's so nice to have friends stay over! Games and . . . games — that's how we'll spend our time."

"I must also report," Rolandus continued, "that the phone lines seem to be down for the moment."

"Gollipops!" said Porculina. "Well, I hope that doesn't . . ."

Suddenly, the room was plunged into darkness. There were a few gasps here and there, and Jumping Bean cried, "Hoorah!"

A moment later, however, a flame flickered up before Rolandus's face. He had struck a match and was lighting a candle he had apparently brought with him. In a moment, the room was bathed in a soft golden glow. "I feared that might happen," said the dog, "so I've already had candles lit in all the sitting rooms and in all of your rooms, as well as in the sconces of the walls in the larger hallways."

"My, but you're the efficient one, aren't ye?" said Woof. "We'd be in a fine fix if ye weren't here."

"But I always am," Rolandus replied mildly. "I'm sorry I didn't keep more of an eye on the weather outside, but my time was somewhat taken up with the banquet. We're a little . . . understaffed just at the moment. Anyway, may I show you all to the sitting room now? I've arranged for hot chocolate to be brought while you wait."

"Lovely," said Gorilla, his good mood unimpaired. "Listen, Roly old boy, could you fetch my bagpipes? Everyone is terribly keen to hear me play."

*   *   *

Later that night, as Teddy lay awake in bed, still shaking at the memory of Gorilla's bagpipes recital, he thought to himself how well all the guests had held up throughout the ordeal. Of course, the strain had been visible on all of their faces — or almost all of them: while everyone else was discreetly attempting to shield his or her ears with a casually raised paw or trotter or webbed foot, Cuttles had sat placidly still, seeming genuinely absorbed in the music. There had been a welcome respite at the end of one long piece called "The Sneezing Cows in the Wee Green Meadow" when Blue Bunny had spoken up to say that he was going to go downstairs to try to start the auxiliary generator and Woof had taken the opportunity to deliver a short lecture on the sad state of the castle's wiring. But Gorilla had resumed playing as soon as he could, performing a tune of his own that he called "The Bonnie Elephants of Perth." There had then been another respite when Rolandus had brought sandwiches and warm milk and encouraged Gorilla to refresh himself; but ten minutes later the Laird had set his plate aside and begun a vigorous rendition of something called "Whither Do You Wander, My Darling Hippo?" Finally — and blessedly — Rolandus had returned to inform Gorilla that it was his bedtime. The Laird of Castle MacGorilla had groaned with disappointment, and all his guests had expressed their own dismay quite movingly, but Gorilla had followed the dog out of the sitting room with no protest. When he had gone, all the guests except Cuttles had breathed deep sighs of relief; then, still shivering, exchanging a few quavery encouragements, they had soon departed for their various beds, the frogs, Woof, and Mr MacAw waiting on the landing until Rolandus returned to show them to their rooms.

Teddy had hoped to fall into a deep sleep quickly, but it was some time before his nerves ceased vibrating from the unearthly wailing of the pipes. At last, though, after almost two hours, he felt himself drifting into unconsciousness, and was just on the verge of deep sleep when he was jolted awake again by a great crashing noise — or rather a great *thump-bump-crash-bang-blast* sort of noise — rising from below. It rolled through the castle like thunder. Instantly, the little bear sat up and felt for the matches and candle that Rolandus had left on the table by his bed. He nearly knocked the table over in his haste, but finally had the candle lit and went to the door. He listened for a moment but heard nothing. Opening the door, he peered out. As he looked up and down the hall, which was still awash in the soft flickering candlelight from the wall sconces, he saw two other doors opening and the heads of Porculina and Woof emerging from behind them.

"What was that sound?" said Porculina in a loud stage whisper.

"I don't know," said Teddy, in much the same voice.

"T' me," said Woof in a more normal tone, "it sounded like it came from daenstairs, wha'ever it was."

"Caramel!" said Porculina, stepping into the hall in her bright pink woolen pajamas with maroon polka dots. "Do you think someone's been hurt? Lost any stuffing or anything?"

"Perhaps we'd better check," said Teddy, smoothing his blue silk pajamas with his free hand. "I'll go down by myself."

"Nay, I'll gang wi' ye," said Woof.

"Let's all go," said Porculina. "It's a little . . . scary with all the lights out."

At just that moment, however, there was the sound of several confident footfalls coming from the direction of the landing, and a few seconds later Gorilla came strolling down the corridor, wearing a white gown and nightcap with golden stripes and carrying a candle in one hand and a blue rubber ball in the other. "I say," he called out cheerfully when he saw the others, "did someone drop something enormously heavy down the stairs? Because I just heard a sort of *thump-bump-crash-bang-blast* noise that nearly shook me out of my bed."

"We all heard it too," said Teddy, "but we don't know what it was." He looked about him. "It doesn't appear to have wakened anyone else."

"Well, the other rooms are further along," said Gorilla, pointing down the hall past Porculina, "around the corner there and on the other side of some doors. I expect no one heard it."

"It was so loud, though," said Porculina.

"Oh, well, it's a big castle," Gorilla said. "If I hadn't been up . . . um, thinking about some very important things, I might not have heard it myself." He glanced down at the ball in his hand and then slipped it quickly into a pocket in his gown.

"We were aboot to go daenstairs an' have a gander," said Woof. "Would ye care to come along?"

"Yes, indeed," said Gorilla, "I'm always up for a good gander."

So the four small toy animals, each carrying a lit candle, made their way to the great central staircase and cautiously down to the main floor. There were no candles lit in the foyer, so it was rather as if they were descending into a vast well of darkness, but they reached the broad, cold floor without stumbling. And then, all at once, they noticed another small flickering light off in the distance, in the sitting room where Gorilla had given his recital hours before, and after a few moments more they were able to make out a shadowy figure holding a candle up in the air and walking about.

"We'd better be very quiet . . ." Teddy began to say.

"Hullo!" Gorilla cried out in his loudest voice. "Who's that there?"

The figure turned around and came out of the sitting room into the foyer. It was Rolandus. "Ah, sir, you're up," he said, and walked over to the party. "Did you perhaps drop something . . . or knock something over . . . or perhaps accidentally overturn a large piece of furniture and cause it to crash down the stairs . . . or anything like that?"

"No," said Gorilla, "not that I recall."

"We heard the noise as well," said Teddy. "That's why we're here."

"Well," said the dog with a puzzled look on his candlelit features, "I had just come up from the basement when it happened. I was down there trying to find Blue, to see why the auxiliary generator wasn't working yet — he wasn't there, though — and just as I got back here I heard that dreadful crash from the sitting room there. At least, that was definitely the direction it came from. But I can't find anything amiss. I thought I'd better just check the treasure room next."

"By all means, yes," said Teddy. "Let's all go have a look."

"Right-o," said Gorilla.

The five of them passed through the sitting room to the green baize door. Rolandus turned the doorknob but, when he pushed, found that the door would not open. "It seems to be bolted," he said.

"But the bolt's on the inside, isn't it?" asked Teddy.

"What does that mean?" asked Porculina.

"Well, it means someone's in there," said the little bear, "unless whoever it was locked the door and then climbed out the window."

Rolandus stared at them for a moment with what seemed an expression of true worry on his face. Then he turned back to the door and knocked on it loudly. "Hello," he called, "is there anybody in there?" There was no response and, after a moment, he knocked again, even more loudly. "I say, is there anyone in there?" For another several moments there was no sound.

Then, however, just as the dog had raised his paw to knock once more, a low, trembling, prolonged moan issued from behind the door: "Oooooohhhwaahhhhh . . . ."

"Barley cakes!" squealed Porculina. "It's a ghost!"

"Oh, we don't have any ghosts here," said Gorilla. "At least, I don't think we do. Do we, Roly?"

"Well, sir," said Rolandus, "none has ever formerly introduced himself."

"And they're very polite as a rule," said Gorilla. "Of course, it might be some other castle's ghost just paying us a visit. A friendly sort of ghost, perhaps."

"Or it might not be a ghost at all," said Teddy. "Either way, we need to get that door open. Can we break it down?"

"It's a stout door," said Rolandus. He knocked again and called out, "Who's there, please?"

After a moment, another moan soaked through the door: "Ohhh . . . wahhhh . . . meee . . . idzmeee . . . I thingggggggg . . . ggmfff . . . ."

"Who's that?" the dog asked again, but now there was no answer, and several more knocks on the door elicited nothing. "Well," Rolandus finally said, "I suppose I could go outside and try to get in through the window. Even if it's locked, it's easier to break a pane of glass than to break down an oak door. The snow stopped falling some while back, but it's deep on the ground, so I'd better fetch some boots. I'll be a few moments. If you don't mind waiting here, miss, sirs, just in case whoever it is tries to come out . . ."

"If these three'll stay," said Woof, "I'll come wi' ye. It may take us both to hoist in over the sill. And, nay, dinna worry aboot boots fer me. M' feet nivver get cold."

The two of them departed and the others waited outside the door. Every now and then, Teddy knocked again and called out to whoever was

41

on the other side, but there was no reply, apart from one faint moan: "Grmfffllermmmm . . ." After a while, he gave up.

So they waited in silence until, after about seven minutes, Gorilla suddenly said, "Do you think that, if it's a ghost, its name might be Henry?"

The other two stared at him in the soft, fluttering, golden light.

"Why would he be called Henry?" asked Porculina. "Is there some legend about a ghost named Henry in these parts?"

"Oh, no," Gorilla replied, "at least not that I've ever heard. I just thought Henry might be a nice name for a ghost."

"Oh," said Porculina.

When fully ten minutes had passed, the three of them heard what could only be the sound of the heavy window sash being lifted in the casement — it obviously had not been used much in recent years, for it squeaked and shuddered mightily as it rose — and then labored grunts and the sound of someone scrambling into the room over the windowsill, and then Woof loudly protesting, "Hey, mind where y' put yer foot noo! I've only got the one head, y' know."

Porculina called out, "Can you see anything?"

"A moment, miss," Rolandus's voice came back through the door, "we're just going to . . . Oh, my goodness!"

"What is it?" called Teddy. "Is anyone hurt?"

"You see to him, Woof," Rolandus could be heard saying, "and I'll let the others in."

Then the three outside heard the bolt sliding back, and the door opened, and they hurriedly pressed forward.

"Over here, sirs, miss, right here." Rolandus was pointing to a figure that lay sprawled upon the floor not far from the fireplace, hardly moving, with Woof kneeling beside it. There was no question whose figure it was; even in the flickering candlelight, everyone immediately recognized the bright electric blue of its fur.

"Easy noo," said Woof gently, "dinna move yet, auld cony."

"Blue!" cried Gorilla. "That's no place for you to sleep. You'll get a stiff back."

"Nay, it's not sleep," said Woof. "Someone's laid him oot cold. It's a good thing his seams are all intact. But that's not all." The toy dog looked up at them with an expression of dismay on his face. "Look over there." He pointed towards the large oval podium.

Everyone turned and stared. It took a moment for them to make out what they were looking at in the dim light, and another moment for what they saw to sink in.

Porculina was the first to speak: "Oh, buttered lemons, the treasure! It's gone!"

Indeed, the podium lay on its side, and nothing of the glorious and resplendent treasure that had been displayed on it — apart from a few scattered rubber balls and a rather forlorn looking paperclip necklace lying limply on the carpet — was visible anywhere. Even the great oil portraits were now absent from the walls, leaving only a few empty hooks and brackets behind.

"Hmm," said Gorilla after a moment, "that's very odd." Then, after another moment, he turned to Rolandus. "Roly, old fellow, this isn't the room where the treasure *isn't*, is it? Or is it the one where the treasure *is*?"

"I fear, sir," replied the dog solemnly, "that this is the room where the treasure *was*, but *isn't* any longer." He pointed to the overturned podium. "As you see. I hate to say it, milord, but your treasure's been stolen."

A perplexed look came over Gorilla's face and he tilted his head to one side thoughtfully. "Now, who could have done that, I wonder? Do you think it might have been Henry?"

Rolandus stared back silently for a few seconds, looking a little nonplussed. "I'm sorry, sir, I don't think I know who Henry is."

"You know," said Gorilla, "the ghost. Henry. Tall chap, with a longish beard and a largish nose and a pleasant smile."

"The . . . ghost, sir?" Then the dog shook his head, as if trying to dislodge something from his ears. "No, sir, I don't think it was Henry, or any ghost at all for that matter. That would be . . . interesting, of course.

But I think we've been the victims of robbers."

"Then again," Teddy remarked quietly, as if puzzling over the matter as he spoke, "at least a ghost might explain how the robbers could have taken the treasure out while leaving the room's door locked from the inside. I suppose they took it out through the window, though."

"Well, no sir," said Rolandus, "that's just the thing. The snow has stopped falling and there's a full moon out and Woof and I could see that the snow under the window was entirely undisturbed. Not a single footprint. No one could have gone that way. And I'm quite sure that that sash hadn't been raised in years, judging from the trouble we had with it."

"Are you absolutely certain?" Teddy asked in a tone of surprise.

"Absolutely."

Gorilla by this time had wandered over to the paperclip necklace and picked it up from the floor. "Well, the silly fellows dropped this, at least." He stroked it almost affectionately and then twisted it double (as it was rather long) and put it around his neck. "Safe and sound," he said.

"But all the rest of the treasure . . ." Porculina said sadly.

"Oh, it'll be back within three days," said Gorilla cheerfully. "Remember the curse. I say, Woof, how's old Blue doing?"

The others turned to see Woof just now helping Blue Bunny to sit up. "Easy, laddie, ye've had a shock. Can ye talk?"

Almost imperceptibly, Blue Bunny nodded, and then leaned his head back on Woof's supporting arm. "I can tallgmmmfff," he said softly.

Suddenly Porculina gasped loudly and clapped her trotters together. "Oh, walnuts!" she cried out happily. "Dollops of whipped cream!"

Everyone except Blue Bunny looked at her.

"Don't you see?" she said, her face and voice ecstatic. "We've had a robbery, from a room that's locked from the inside, with no idea whatsoever how the thief made his getaway! And you're a detective, Teddy! Oh, this is marvelous! We're in a mystery story! This is the most exciting thing that's ever happened to me — absolutely ever! Walnuts! Toasted almonds!" She positively hopped with joy.

CHAPTER 4

A Hidden Door

TWENTY MINUTES LATER, ALL OF THEM WERE back in the sitting room outside the treasure room. Teddy had asked that no one touch anything, so that he could investigate the scene when he had more light to work with. Woof and Rolandus had helped Blue Bunny up onto his feet, and the rabbit had managed to walk with only a little help to a large divan, where he then gently collapsed, resting his head back against its velvet plush. Rolandus had fetched him a glass, a pitcher of carrot juice, and a large platter of fresh carrots and lettuce from the kitchen. Then, eating and drinking slowly but steadily, Blue Bunny had gradually regained some of his strength and all of his senses. As he ate, the others arranged themselves in their chairs, forming a semicircle before him; and only when he seemed sufficiently revived did Teddy look at him with his best grave and thoughtful face and say, "Now, Mr Bunny, are you able to tell us what happened?"

"Well, I suppose so, sir," Blue Bunny said weakly, his nose quivering pathetically, "but I'm afraid I didn't see very much."

"Oh, oh, oh," Gorilla interjected, suddenly very excited, "let me ask the next question! I know just what to ask!"

"Really, Gor-Gor," said Porculina, "Teddy's the expert here."

"But, I really do know what to ask. Oh, please!"

Teddy looked uncertain for a moment, but then shrugged his shoulders. "It's your castle," he said.

"Right-o," said Gorilla, and he turned to the rabbit with an extremely serious look in his eyes. "Blue, this is very important. Did you happen to notice anyone stealing the treasure after you'd gone to bed in the treasure room? Think carefully."

"Well . . ." Blue Bunny looked somewhat confused. "Not exactly. In fact, I didn't actually go to bed . . ."

But Gorilla could not contain himself. "Did you perhaps see a . . ." — he leaned forward eagerly — "well, a ghost, maybe? Perhaps one with a rather longish beard and largish nose and probably a rather kindly smile on his face?"

For several seconds, the rabbit merely stared back at Gorilla in bewildered silence.

"He might have been called Henry," Gorilla added helpfully.

"No, no," Teddy intervened, "really, old fellow, we'll only get off on a false trail if we proceed like that. Honestly, there's a proper method for questioning. Let me do it, please."

Gorilla looked somewhat abashed. "All right," he said with a shrug, "I was only trying to get to the heart of the matter quickly."

46

"Mr Bunny," Teddy resumed, "Blue, what happened? Take your time."

"Well, sir," Blue Bunny replied, his nose beginning to twitch anxiously and the customary wild look returning to his eyes, "my nerves are a bit a-jangle, but I'll try. It doesn't take much time to tell, I'm afraid. I'd just come up from the basement. I hadn't had any luck with the generator, and I came into this room to see if there were still any of those sandwiches that Rolandus had said he was going to bring from the kitchen, and I suddenly heard a terrific crashing and clamor — a sort of *thump-crash-bump-blast-bang* kind of noise." He suddenly sat up, nose furiously twitching, almost as if he had mistaken the sound of his own voice for a repetition of the noise, then he slumped back again, shaking. "It was frightful," he moaned.

"Hmm," said Gorilla, lightly tapping his fingertips together and knitting his brows, "are you quite sure it wasn't more of a sort of *thump-bump-crash-bang-blast* kind of noise?"

"Yes," said Porculina, "that's certainly what we heard."

"Well . . ." The rabbit rubbed his head. "Maybe. I'm a bit boggled just now. Please, sir, I'm doing my very best . . ."

"And doing very well," said Teddy kindly.

The rabbit looked at the little bear with an expression of grateful feebleness. "Anyway," he continued, "whatever kind of sound it was, I was right here when I heard it, so I ran to the door and threw it open and entered the room and I caught a glimpse of an electric torch shining right at me, but before I could see anything else something came down on my head and the next thing I knew I heard someone knocking on the door."

"You saw nothing?" asked Teddy. "Nothing at all?"

"Nothing," said Blue Bunny with a melancholy shake of his head, "not even a shadow. I never saw who was holding the torch, or even what shape he was."

"You saw the light in front of you, but you were hit from behind — is that right?"

Blue Bunny hesitated for a moment, as if reviewing the episode in his mind, and then yelped. "Yes, . . . yes, sir . . ." — his voice had its normal, slightly frantic edge to it now — "So . . . I suppose there must have been two of them. Oh, that's terrifying!"

"Or more than two," said Teddy. "But we could have guessed that. A treasure that size would have been quite a task for a single thief. Could you tell if the treasure was still there when you went in?"

"Not even that, sir. There wasn't time."

"I must have been right behind you coming upstairs," said Rolandus. "I was just coming into the foyer when I heard all that clatter."

"You see," said Teddy, speaking now very clearly and carefully, "the door was locked from the inside and no one went out through the window. You see what that means, don't you?"

"What?" asked Porculina.

"It makes it look," said Teddy, still speaking to Blue Bunny, "as if you were the only person who could have locked the door. Now, that's one mystery. But there's another as well, because if the treasure wasn't taken out the window, it's hard to see how it could have been taken out at all."

"Aye, it's true enough," Woof observed. "There wasna any trace of anything in the snow ootside the window, and that window hadn't been opened in an age, I'd warrant, just as auld Rolandus says."

"Yet there'd have been no way to get the treasure out through this room after you were hit on the head," Teddy continued, "because Rolandus was only moments behind you and would have seen anyone coming out this way. And with that huge load of treasure . . . well, it's just not possible. So, you see, maybe the treasure was already gone, and whoever was in there was looking about for anything that might have been missed, and one of the thieves accidentally knocked over the pedestal, which caused you to come running in. That still doesn't explain the locked door, of course, or tell us when the treasure was taken, or where, but . . ."

Rolandus cleared his throat. "Excuse me, sir, but no, that can't be quite right."

Teddy turned his head. "Why not?"

48

"Because, sir," said the dog, "the sound was not the sound of a single large object striking the floor. I was close enough to hear it clearly, and it was a sound composed of many distinct parts: there were the sounds of things breaking, perhaps china, and then things clattering, with a heavy metallic crash, and almost a sound like something tumbling along a stone corridor or . . . down a flight of distant stairs."

"Stairs?" said Teddy in a mystified tone. "A corridor?"

"Jellies!" said Porculina. "Whatever could that mean? You don't think . . . " she hesitated and looked about her with widening eyes.

"Yes?" asked Teddy after a moment.

"You don't think the thieves brought a flight of stairs with them, do you, Teddykins?"

Teddy sighed and then smiled kindly at his friend. "Well, no, I wouldn't say that sounds very likely. I mean, I've never encountered anything quite like that in any of my former cases. A ladder, maybe . . . "

"Do you think a rhinoceros might have stolen the treasure?" Gorilla suddenly asked, clapping his hands to the sides of his spherical little head.

For a moment, no one said anything.

"I mean," Gorilla continued, warming to the theme, "that would certainly explain the noise. Rhinoceroses always make an awful lot of noise, I should imagine."

"That *is* true," said Porculina.

"That would be something, wouldn't it?" Gorilla said. "I mean, I don't fancy there are many rhinoceroses out robbing Scottish castles."

"Yes," said Teddy raising both his paws in the air before him, as if trying to bring everything to a halt, "that's an interesting theory, I'll grant, but a rhinoceros would have had an even harder time sneaking out of the treasure room unnoticed than a normal robber would. And he certainly would have left tracks in the snow if he'd gone out the window. And it wouldn't explain how the treasure could just . . . well, just vanish, just minutes after making all that clamor."

Gorilla frowned and his eyes narrowed pensively for a moment. Then all at once his expression brightened. "Well, then, that leaves only Henry.

We should have known."

Teddy bowed his head. "Gorilla, old ape, I don't want to be contrary, but I really don't think there is any Henry. And I think we're getting a bit off track."

"Oh," said Gorilla, looking a little crestfallen. Then, tapping his fingers together again and pursing his lips, he gazed down at his toes and murmured, "Reggie, maybe? A ghost might be called Reggie."

Teddy groaned softly.

"Those carrots look absolutely scrumptious," said Porculina to Blue Bunny. "Were you going to eat them all?"

*　　*　　*

Teddy soon decided that nothing more of value could be learned from the rabbit that night. He would dearly have loved to call for the local police, but he had no way of doing so; so long as the phones were out of order and the roads were impassable, he would have to conduct the investigation himself. More to the point, there was probably no time to spare. If the treasure had been taken within the last hour, which seemed to be the only conjecture consistent with everyone's story, then the thieves might very well still be on the grounds, or even in the castle itself. "Have you got any flashlights — I mean, torches?" he asked Rolandus.

"Quite a few, in fact," the dog replied, "but I've been concentrating on keeping candles lit. I assumed the auxiliary generator would be working."

"Yes, well," said Teddy, "if you could get as many flash . . . — as many *torches* as you can, I'd like to see what I can make of the treasure room."

"With your leave," said Rolandus, "I'll just get Blue settled in his bed first."

"If you could, put him in one of the guest rooms, please," said Teddy. "I'll want to explore the grounds next, if I can, and I don't want any unnecessary footprints between the castle and the guardhouse."

So Rolandus and Woof, supporting Blue Bunny between them, guided the rabbit through the dimly lit immensity of the front hall and up the great flight of stairs and off to the rooms above. While the others waited, Porculina devoured the remaining carrots, Gorilla lay upon his back on the divan tossing his blue rubber ball into the air and catching it (usually as it bounced off his stomach), and Teddy paced back and forth across the sitting room, glancing here and there for whatever clues he might be able to discern among the shadows (he found none). At one point, he stepped on Gorilla's bagpipes, which emitted a loud ghastly wail in several pitches at once, causing Gorilla to sit up suddenly and happily call out, "Henry!" Then, however, realizing his mistake, he lay back again and said, "Sorry, Teddy."

After some time, the two dogs returned, carrying seven identical steel-cased flashlights between them. Teddy relieved them of five. "Do you think you two could go downstairs again and see if you can get that generator working?" he asked. "I'm going to begin looking around, but I really do need more light."

"Aye, we can do that," said Woof.

"Certainly, sir," Rolandus added.

When the dogs had gone, Teddy gave Gorilla and Porculina each a flashlight. After convincing Gorilla to stop switching his on and off rapidly and sweeping its beam wildly around the room while making noises reminiscent of a car engine or car horn — not to mention one cry of "Watch out for that tree!" followed by the sound of screeching tires — he asked them to follow him into the treasure room and stand by the door, shining their lights to either side. Then he took two of the three remaining flashlights and positioned them on the floor so as to fan their light out across the room from opposite angles. Then he lit the three candles he found standing on the mantelpiece of the large fireplace and, with the remaining flashlight, began making his careful and gradual examination of the entire room.

"Digestive biscuits, but this is exciting!" Porculina said at one point.

"*Vroom, vroom,*" Gorilla remarked quietly, but he held his flashlight steady. "*Beep.*"

After several minutes of intense scrutiny of the carpet, Teddy finally stopped by the fireplace and raised his head. "All right, I think you two can come over and see what I've found."

Gorilla and Porculina quickly crossed the room to Teddy's side.

"Look here," the little bear said, pointing downward.

On the floor lay the shattered remains of several of the lovely Chinese vases from the mantelpiece.

"Oh, vinegar and bitter milk!" said Porculina. "Your beautiful porcelains! I'm so sorry, Gor-Gor."

"Why, did you break them?" Gorilla asked.

"No, of course not," replied Porculina. "I mean I'm sorry to see them ruined."

Gorilla gazed for a moment at the scattered fragments and then nodded soberly. "They *were* very pretty," he said. Then, however, he glanced down at the paperclip chain hanging from his neck and gave it a gentle stroke. "Things could have been far worse, though."

"I'm sorry too," said Teddy, "but do you see what this means?"

Porculina and Gorilla both shook their heads.

"Well, neither do I, really," said the bear, "but it's curious. The treasure was kept nowhere near here, and neither the door nor the window is nearby, and this old fireplace is too solid to shake very easily, and the mantelpiece is too high to knock things off of through mere carelessness."

"Could the treasure have been carried up the chimney?" asked Porculina.

"No," said Teddy leaning over and shining his torch up through the flue, "it's too narrow, and there's no sign of anything going up this way — scattered ashes or anything. It would be a nice explanation for the locked door and window, if it were possible, but no," — he straightened up again — "it's not possible. Nothing could get all that treasure up there."

At Teddy's request, the other two resumed their station by the door, and the bear continued his painstaking exploration of every inch of the room. "If only the lights were on," he muttered now and then. Finally, after several voyages around the carpet, he returned to the mantel again, leaning over first to inspect the mouth of the chimney and then the bricks at the back of the fireplace itself. "Gorilla," he said, "have you ever noticed that one of these bricks protrudes a bit from the wall?"

Gorilla and Porculina came over to Teddy's side again.

"Right here," said Teddy, pointing the beam of his flashlight at a brick well above the level of the grate, at a place at the back of the fireplace that would normally be hidden in shadows when the lights were on. "Have you noticed that before?"

"Maybe," said Gorilla, "when I was a little ape and used to play in here. I never gave it much notice if I did. Why, do you like bricks? If you fancy that one, you can have it."

"Well, no, that's not why I mention it," said Teddy. "It doesn't look like just a loose brick. It looks like I could just press it in and . . ." — he leaned down again — "and maybe there'd be a spring behind it. Are there any stories about, oh, hidden passages or secret hiding places?"

"Oh, loads of them," said Gorilla, "stories and stories. My illustrated ancestors were all in favor of secret hiding places and passages, in case the castle was attacked and they had to hide the treasure or escape, or if they wanted to play hide and seek, or any of the other things hidden passages are good for. You know, like bowling. They say Angus MacGorilla built six or seven of them, just to hide the treasure hoard in an emergency, but I never really paid much attention to the details."

"Well," said Teddy, with a mild look of exasperation on his face, "don't you think that might explain a thing or two?"

"Oh, I don't know," said Gorilla. "I don't think these solid old stones have hidden passages behind them." He patted the wall to the left of the fireplace and leaned against it with a casual air. "It would be exciting, of course, but I'd have come across them by now if they were there. Well, unless they were hidden or something."

"Oh, but this is just too thrilling for words," Porculina said. "What if there really is a secret room or passage? It really is just like one of my mystery novels."

"Look," said Teddy, reaching into the fireplace, "I'm just going to give it a try and we'll see . . ." and he pressed the protruding brick very lightly, and almost at once it gave way. There was the sound of a spring releasing somewhere in the wall beside the fireplace, the mantelpiece shuddered violently, and suddenly the portion of the wall upon which Gorilla was leaning swung back with a moan of grinding stone and iron, and Gorilla tumbled backwards out of sight, dropping his flashlight on the carpet as he fell.

"Crumpets!" Porculina exclaimed. "Oh, Teddy, Gorilla's been eaten by the wall. Gor-Gor, are you all right?" She trotted over to the opening in the wall, peering into the darkness, but not thinking to shine her light ahead of her. "Apey-Wapey, dear, are you there? Yoo-hoo!"

When there was no immediate reply, Teddy also called out, "Old fellow, are you all right?"

"Hmm . . ." Gorilla's voice floated to them out of the darkness, now accompanied by a faint stony echo. "You know, Teddy, I think I may have found what you were looking for. Was it a dark and empty sort of not-thereness? Just about where one might expect the wall to be standing?"

Teddy crossed quickly to Porculina's side, picking up Gorilla's flashlight as he did so, and then aimed it along with his own into the darkness beyond the opening in the wall. "Pigsy," he said, "could you aim your light forward?"

"Oh, yes," she said absently, raising her hand.

In the three broad beams of light, Gorilla could be seen lying on his back, staring upward with a strangely unconcerned look on his face, looking almost serene in his gown and nightcap. Beyond his form, a dark corridor with plain walls and a low ceiling of old rust-red and dull blue brick stretched away into deeper shadows.

"Hullo," said Gorilla after a moment. "Fancy finding this here. It's really rather comfortable — except for whatever's poking into my back."

Porculina breathed in deeply and then whistled softly. "This is absolutely fantabulous!" she said. "Oh, Teddy, it gives me goosefabric. It makes me absolutely . . . well, absolutely . . . peckish."

"Gorilla," said Teddy, "do you think you might want to get up?"

Gorilla considered this for a moment. "I suppose so," he said, "but I'm trying to tell what it is that's poking me in the back."

"If you got up, you could just look and see," said Teddy.

Again Gorilla seemed to be considering. "I suppose I could," he said after a moment, and sat up and, with Teddy's assistance, rose to his feet. Then he took back his flashlight, turned, stooped over, and said, "Well, well, fancy that!" He stood up again, now holding something in his paw. "It's a piece of jewelry, a — what are they called — a thingummy — you know, a roach, a diamond roach."

"A *roach?*" said Porculina, with a distinct tone of distaste in her voice.

"Yes, you know, a gemmy sort of thing that you pin on your blouse. I suppose it's called that because it's a little like a large insect. It has diamonds all over . . ."

"A broach," said Teddy, "he means a broach. Can I see it?"

"Certainly," said Gorilla, handing it over.

Teddy examined it closely. It was an exquisitely finely wrought piece of jewelry, shaped to look like a peacock with its tail outspread, brightly enameled in numerous hues, and encrusted all around its edges with small, brilliant diamonds. "Is this a piece from your treasure hoard?" he asked.

"Oh, yes," said Gorilla, "that one used to be worn by my Aunt Selena occasionally, and I used to play zoo with it, along with the other pieces that looked like animals. I wonder how it got here."

"Well, isn't that obvious?" said Porculina.

"It seems this was definitely the way the thieves got the treasure out," said Teddy. "It also explains how the door could have been locked from the inside. But it means that your thieves must have known of this secret passage somehow. And it also means they were in a hurry to get out of here. Professional thieves, working carefully, would never let anything this lovely escape their notice."

"Well, then," said Porculina, "what next?"

"I suppose I have to explore this corridor," said the little bear, placing the broach on the mantelpiece. "The robbery was no more than an hour ago, and the criminals might still be on grounds. That was a great deal of treasure to be hauling; they can't just have dashed away. And in all this snow they can't drive off with it in a car. In fact, I can't imagine why they would have chosen a night like this for their theft . . ."

"You can't go on your own!" Porculina suddenly cried out. "These are desperate villains, Teddykins. Think of poor Blue Bunny."

"Yes," said Teddy, "I know, but I'll be careful. There may still be time to catch them. Look, you go and get Rolandus and Woof, and I'll start the search."

"No," said Porculina firmly, "if you're going now, we're going with you too."

"Right she is," said Gorilla cheerfully. "One for all and six or one half-dozen for the other! Fluffy friends forever!" He raised a finger in the air, clearly taking encouragement from the sound of his own voice. "Keep a candle burning! A stitch in time saves limes! Here we go round the mulberry . . ."

"Yes, all right," said Teddy, somewhat impatiently. Then, in a gentler tone, he added, "I suppose I'd feel safer with my two best friends along. But please keep behind me, and be ready to run back the way you came if danger appears."

So the three of them made their way along the passage, Teddy in the lead, followed by Porculina, with Gorilla bringing up the rear. They moved quickly but carefully, shining their flashlights before them and to either side. The hallway was practically featureless, and the bare walls ran straight ahead, with only some empty torch brackets in the walls here and there. "This is very old," Teddy observed at one point. "Maybe mediaeval."

"It's pretty grim too," said Porculina.

"*Chugga-chugga, chugga-chugga, choo-chooooo,*" added Gorilla quietly, though more to himself than to his companions; then, a few seconds later, he added, "Once more onto the beach, dear fiends . . ."

"We have to concentrate, Gor-Gor," said Porculina.

After nearly five minutes, the end of the passage came into view: a brick wall with a single iron ring, about the size of a bell-pull handle, hanging from an iron socket at its center. The three came to a halt.

"Well," said Teddy, "I assume that's a handle that opens a door."

"Golly," said Porculina, "shall we pull it?"

"Are you two sure you want to come with me?" asked Teddy.

"Definitely," said Gorilla, "no matter what we find — be it a ghost, a rhinoceros, or something wholly unexpected . . . like a gang of leopards in top hats, or anything like that."

Teddy looked at his friends for a moment, and then said, "Well, all right, but remember, be careful and quiet." Then he took hold of the iron ring and turned it, now one way and now the other. Nothing happened. Breathing deeply, he pulled back on it. Again nothing. Finally, he took hold of it again and turned and pulled it at once, first to the left, then to the right. There was a sort of loud creak, followed by the sound of something grinding — rather as though a large set of gears were turning and chains were clanking — and the wall moved, slowly, groaningly swinging open and inward at its left side, moving on some large hidden hinge at its right. Immediately, a cold, fresh breeze blew through the opening, and a pale silvery light spilled into the corridor.

The three friends stepped back as the door swung all the way open, and they saw spread out before them the east grounds of the castle, stretching away from the wall and down a slight incline to a broad open lawn and some distant ornamental garden gates, beyond which stood the topiary maze. The blizzard had passed, but had transformed everything. In place of the emerald grass there was a sea of white, in which the snow-capped tops of the gateposts seemed to float like jetsam and out of which the snow-crested barberry hedges of the maze's imposing outer wall seemed to rise like a great wave. The whole scene glimmered with an almost magical loveliness under a clear starry sky and a brilliant full moon.

"Gooseberries!" whispered Porculina. "It's like a dream."

Teddy nodded. Then, as his eyes adjusted to the shimmering white world outside, he pointed first downward and then up and away again towards the maze, as if following something in movement. "Look," he said, "tracks. There are large tracks in the snow."

The others looked. There were indeed tracks in the snow, starting just below the castle wall and proceeding across the grounds in a slightly

57

elliptical path, down the incline toward the distant barberry hedges. They were very strange tracks, moreover: extremely large, and shaped almost like large teardrops, the rounded ends all aiming away from the castle.

"They're gigantic!" gasped Porculina. "Maybe it was a rhinoceros, after all. Though I don't think that's really what a rhino print looks like..."

"That settles it," said Gorilla, "it was a whale...or a dragon."

"Do whales have feet...?" Porculina began.

"A dragon, then," Gorilla said with an air of firm finality.

"No, no," said Teddy, "I've seen those sorts of tracks before, and what they mean is that this thief was prepared. Those are the prints made by snowshoes, and they aren't very deep, so I don't think anyone huge was wearing them. If you look closely, maybe in the morning, you'll probably see some cross-hatching in the prints." He paused for a moment, quietly clicking his tongue. "Here's where we split up, I think. I'll follow the tracks and you..."

"No," said Porculina resolutely, "we go forward together or we go back together. It's just not safe, Teddykins. You could get knocked down, or have snow thrown at you, or anything."

Teddy paused again, staring ahead of him, rubbing his paws together and shivering slightly. "All right," he said at last, "if we're careful we might be able to see where the thief has gone. Turn your flashlights off but keep them with you. The moonlight is more than bright enough. We might even be able to sneak up on him—or her—or them. But, whatever else we do, please remember to be absolutely qui..."

"Hullo!" Gorilla suddenly shouted at the top of his voice. "Who's out there, please? And did you take my treasure?"

Teddy's chin sank to his chest and he heaved a doleful sigh. "I think we may have lost the element of surprise," he said.

CHAPTER 5

A Chase in the Dark

"WELL," TEDDY REMARKED A FEW MOMENTS later, "we might as well be deliberate about this now."

He led the other two back along the hallway, through the treasure room, through the sitting room, and into the great foyer. He was about to ask the way to the basement, in order to find Rolandus and Woof, when the two dogs entered the foyer from the other side. In as few words as he could, and despite Gorilla's occasional interjections about whales and dragons, Teddy quickly explained what he, Porculina, and Gorilla had found. Woof was surprised but Rolandus was positively astonished: in all the generations that his family had been in service to the castle, he said, none of them had ever stumbled across a hidden passage. Teddy urged him not to worry about that now, however, but to find some boots for everyone so that the five of them could form a search party immediately. "Time is still on our side," he said.

It took only a few minutes for Rolandus to return from the servants' quarters downstairs with his arms full. With his customary efficiency, he had managed to find a small pair of pink boots that fitted Porculina's trotters perfectly and a serviceable pair of black boots that suited Teddy well enough. He also brought Gorilla's favorite pair of bright purple Wellingtons, as well as warm red and blue woolen scarves for everyone.

Woof also departed briefly, only to return with a particularly ferocious looking wrench he had fetched from his toolbox. "Aye, weel, we'll see," he said. "If there's any noggin to be bashed, it willna be mine."

"Oh, jellies!" said Porculina.

"Aye, miss," said Woof, "I dinna fancy having my stuffing knocked aboot."

Once properly attired, the five of them made their way back to the treasure room and from there down the passageway and out into the night.

"Those tracks," Rolandus said after a moment surveying the snow, "are rather extraordinary, aren't they?"

"Whale tracks," Gorilla said with authority.

"Snowshoes, to be precise," said Teddy.

In the brilliant moonlight, it was easy to follow the prints, and the party moved as swiftly as they could through the deep snow with their flashlights switched off. It was obvious even before they began that the path led down towards the topiary maze, but it was not until they reached the towering outer hedge that they saw that the tracks went directly in through the arched opening in the hedge wall.

60   "Why would they have gone that way?" asked Rolandus.

"Perhaps they didn't know what it was," Teddy said, peering into the maze. "Or maybe they did. Is there another way out?"

"I've never been able to tell," said Gorilla.

"Yes," Rolandus said, "at the other side. But it's not easy to find, unless one already knows the way."

"Well, then," said Teddy, "we may just have our quarry trapped. All right, everyone, be careful." And with that he entered the maze, turning on his flashlight as he did so.

"Right-ho," said Gorilla enthusiastically, "Up the hill, over the barricades! Thar she blows! Don't feed the seals! Don't tease the stoats!" And he too entered, followed by Porculina, then Woof, and finally Rolandus.

The five paused just within the opening. In stark contrast to the gleaming crystalline beauty of the snow-covered lawns, here all seemed dark, mysterious, and forbidding. The high hedges whelmed everything in inky shadow, the paths between them were narrow, and every gap in them seemed to open into impenetrable gloom. In the light of the flashlights, however, the search party could see the same teardrop footprints running before them in a straight line ahead, along the main way from the maze's entrance, and so they began to follow. Soon, however, they reached a place where the path opened out into a small circular courtyard awash in moonlight, at whose center stood the immense figure of a centaur with a drawn bow.

"This is a sculpture garden as well," Rolandus quietly remarked, "in case you were unaware."

"Oh, no," said Porculina, "look at the footprints now!"

And, in fact, here the path dissolved into a chaos of crisscrossing tracks: tracks doubling back, tracks in circles, tracks going into various openings in the circular wall of the courtyard and coming out again. There were also a few large indentations in the snow where someone had apparently fallen over and then struggled to get up again.

"Someone appears to be lost," said Teddy. "We should post someone back at the gate we came through and then the rest of us had better split up and . . ."

"There!" cried Porculina, pointing ahead of her. "There's someone right over there, on the other side, right in the shadow of the hedge, holding something over his head . . . a sort of . . . scimitar or something!"

Everyone looked intently. Woof slowly raised his wrench and took a step forward.

"That's nothing," Rolandus said. "It's a statue. I'm afraid there are quite a few of them in here. That one is of a famous MacGorilla — Ewan MacGorilla, in fact — successor to Angus as Laird of the Castle. The object he's holding in the air is, in fact . . ." He paused.

"A banana?" asked Teddy after a moment. "A very large banana?"

Rolandus nodded. "Yes, sir. I'm afraid it is. You seem, sir, to have . . . ah, got the hang of this place."

"Don't be afraid," said Gorilla. "Bananas never harmed a soul."

"Anyway," the bear said, "we have to find our thief before he finds the way out at the other end. Pigsy, you have the shrillest voice among us — or, um, that is to say, the clearest and . . . sweetest — so do you think you could go back and watch the entrance? Stay out of sight, in the shadows of the first break in the main path. If the thief doubles back, don't try to catch him, just wait till he passes, then give a mighty cry, and we'll all come running. In this snow, he won't be able to run any faster than anyone else, I imagine, and we'll get him."

"Oh, that's no fun," the pig protested. "I want to be one of the hunters, not a boring old sentry. You just think my legs are too short for a chase through all this snow."

Teddy cleared his throat a little guiltily. "Please," he said, "that's the way out the thief definitely already knows about. We need a sentry, with a loud clear voice, and . . . and you really have the loudest . . . tones."

"You mean 'squeal,' don't you?" she asked, a little petulantly. "Oh, all right, Teddykins, but, if we catch him, I get to say," — she suddenly lowered her voice, clearly attempting to sound a little menacing — "'Ho ho, my good fellow, you thought you could escape justice, but justice is the swiftest thing of all!' I want to say it just like that: 'Ho ho, my good fellow, you thought you could . . .'"

"Yes, yes, of course," said Teddy, "I promise. But please, time is ticking away."

Porculina shrugged, turned on her trotters, and headed back the way they had come.

"Now," said the little bear to the others, "these tracks are completely unreadable, so we have to try to be as systematic as our thief has been erratic."

"Yes, indeed," said Gorilla. "I'm not sure what that means, but it sounds very impressive to me."

"Remember," Teddy continued, "if you find our quarry, call out for help and wave the beam of your flashlight overhead so the rest of us can try to get to where you are. Keep calling, and don't feel you have to apprehend the criminal by yourself. He's not necessarily very big — his tracks aren't very deep, after all — but he clearly has a nasty disposition."

Rolandus and Woof nodded solemnly, but Gorilla cleared his throat, leaned over, and whispered in Teddy's ear: "I don't want to embarrass you, old fellow, but there isn't really any quarry around here. This is a garden, you see."

"Yes, yes," said Teddy aloud, patting Gorilla on the shoulder, "I don't mean that kind of quarry. I meant the thief we're chasing. The quarry in the hunt, so to speak. Look, I'll take this path to the right, you go to the left, Woof will go over to the one at the left end of the courtyard, and Rolandus to the one at the right end. Is everyone agreed?"

The dogs both nodded again and Gorilla said, "Tally-ho!" Then, glancing around, he added, "Remember Robert the Bruce!" Then he turned and walked away to the left, uttering a parting "Sing a song of sixpence!" as he did so.

"Now," said Teddy, turning to the other two, "let's get moving. And remember: be careful."

*   *   *

Gorilla was not exactly furtive as he made his way now around one bend in the maze and then another. He strode through the snow as vigorously as he could, hummed softly to himself through smiling lips, and swung his flashlight from side to side with a sort of gallant carelessness. Now and then, he uttered a soft airplane engine's noise and a very quiet "Look out for that mountain." Every once in a while, he called out softly, "Hullo, out there," or "Are you there, Mr Thief?" or "Here Whalie-Whalie-Whalie," or "Henry?" But he received no reply. On several occasions, he came upon the tall moon-silvered silhouette of one or another large figure with some fearsome object raised above its head (banana, garden hoe, balloon animal, giant lollipop), and leapt back or even cried out before he realized it was yet another statue.

The first time this happened, it was a statue of a particularly celebrated MacGorilla, Harold Ironpaws, holding a toy sword aloft, and Gorilla let out such a little yell of surprise that Teddy's anxious voice immediately came floating over the hedges: "Gorilla, old fellow, what's wrong? Are you all right?"

"Oh, just one of the illustrated figures from MacGorilla clan history," Gorilla shouted back. "He sort of came on me in the darkness — if you know what I mean."

After a moment, Teddy's reply came back: "All right, then."

Gorilla did his best to follow the tracks in the snow, although they seemed to lead nowhere — or, rather, they seemed to lead everywhere, veering from one path to another, doubling back, roving in circles, dissolving in a frantic back-and-forth. But he dutifully tried to follow where they led. "Dear, dear," he said to himself at one point, "if this is a whale, he's clearly not very steady on his toes. Or flukes, I suppose."

Suddenly a massive form, holding what seemed to be a large stone up over its head, seemed to loom out of the shadows at him. "I say!" he cried, and thrust his flashlight out in front of him defensively as he took two steps back and fell over in the snow. But it was only a statue of a giant caterpillar stretching up from the ground to eat a large cherry dangling from an invisible bough.

* * *

Teddy meanwhile was taking a somewhat more deliberate approach to his pursuit of the thief. He too was trying to follow a mad whirligig of crisscrossing tracks, but was beginning to get a sense of the general course the thief had taken. Moving along the narrow paths, his way only fitfully lit by the moonlight, his flashlight illuminating only a few feet of ground before him and seeming to deepen the shadows beyond its beam, he had managed to determine that the thief was alone — there was only one set of snowshoe prints — and had gone to the right from the open courtyard, become hopelessly confused, and had finally found his way back along the path by which he had come. "Wherever he is," the little bear concluded to himself, "he's back there, behind me somewhere."

At just that moment, he came around a corner and was momentarily brought up short before a statue of a porpoise dancing upright on its tail with a ball balanced on its snout. He did not cry out, but he was nearly as startled as Gorilla might have been. He was less surprised a few moments later when he came across another statue, this time of a gorilla mounted on a rocking horse and wearing a cowboy hat. "That's surely not Angus," he said. He stared at it a moment longer, wondering whether there were not something hauntingly familiar about this gorilla's profile, but then moved on. He was not even mildly alarmed when he came upon the next statue, that of a dragon eating buttered toast. At last he found his way back to the path leading to the courtyard.

*   *   *

Porculina waited patiently near the castle-side opening to the maze, keeping out of sight just inside the first opening leading off from the main path, as Teddy had asked. She was bored and she was hungry. It was about that time of early morning when she generally awoke for a small snack or two before returning to her bed for a few hours more. "Oh, golly, this is vexing!" she muttered at one point.

Now and then, she quietly practiced her "Ho ho, my good fellow, you thought you could escape justice, but justice is the swiftest thing of all!"

Sometimes she tried it in the deepest voice she could manage, sometimes in a slightly higher, more cutting voice, and now and then the tedium of waiting caused her to mix the words up, and to say things like "Good fellow, ho ho, you thought justice could escape you, but you are the swiftest . . ."

She sighed.

After a while, when still nothing had happened, she bent down and gathered some snow into a small pile and began to fashion it into a little snowpig. It was really rather pretty.

*　　*　　*

Teddy reached the courtyard almost at the same moment as Rolandus and, just as the two of them were walking towards one another to confer, Woof also arrived. Teddy told them both what he had determined from the prints over in the corner of the maze he had investigated.

"Well, I can report much the same thing," said Rolandus. "The other entrance lies at the end I was exploring, but I could tell from the tracks that our thief never found his way out. He got lost and wandered about for a while and then finally headed back this way."

"Aye," said Woof, "the same wi' me. In and aroond and back and forth and then oot again. Ye'll nae find him that way."

Teddy nodded thoughtfully and then, without saying a word, began to move all around the courtyard, following the tracks in the snow as well as he could, going around the great figure of the centaur no fewer than four times, and at last returning to the two dogs with his jaws firmly clenched. "I think we can lay out the course he took," he said after a few seconds. With his flashlight, he pointed out each stage of the thief's journey as he spoke: "He came in by the main path, reached the courtyard, and first took a right and went down the way I explored, then came out again and tried the quarter Rolandus covered, then came out again and tried Woof's quarter, then came out again and . . ." He stopped, his flashlight now directed towards the opening that Gorilla had taken when the four of them had gone their several ways. Teddy, Rolandus, and Woof looked at one another with expressions of forlorn worry spreading over each of their faces. Then, without saying a word, they all three began to dash madly in the direction in which Teddy had just been pointing.

* * *

Gorilla had come to a pause in a small circular clearing in the maze where one path branched off into three others. He had already ventured down each of them only to find that the tracks led back to this point again in each case. "I don't know," he said with a deep breath and a perplexed narrowing of his eyes. He reached under his nightcap and scratched his head. "I can't tell where he went. It all seems to come back to here." He looked around the clearing, swinging his flashlight. Nothing was moving in the moonlight, and the beam of his flashlight revealed nothing in the shadows below the hedges. He examined the tracks in the snow again, but again could make no sense of them. He shrugged, raised his head, and began to walk back toward the path that had originally brought him here.

He momentarily hesitated, however, when he noticed yet another motionless figure in silhouette, brandishing yet another object of some sort over its head, standing near the place where he had first entered the clearing. He did not jump or cry out this time, though; he had resolved by this point not to be frightened by any more statues. Instead he smiled, strode over to the figure, looked up into its indiscernible eyes, laughed knowingly, and said, "No, you won't get me this time, old stone-face. So" — he turned around and looked back over the clearing — "where do *you* think our robber's got to, ay?"

At that moment, the figure shifted, turned towards the unsuspecting Gorilla, and brought the object in its hand down upon the nightcapped head with a soft but distinct *thonk*.

Gorilla was surprised. "Oh," he said softly. After a moment, he realized what had happened, but could not at first recall what was generally supposed to happen next in situations like this. "Ouch! Oh, ouch! Dearie me!" he yelled very loudly, not so much because he felt any need to, but because he was still thinking and wanted to avoid any awkward silence while he was doing so. Then he remembered what to do and, ever eager to do his part, promptly collapsed face-forward in the snow. After a few moments he began to snore contentedly.

The figure waited for a few seconds and then quietly sneaked away.

* * *

When he awoke again, Gorilla found himself back in the sitting room where only hours before he had been merrily entertaining his guests with his bagpipes. Now the room was quiet and he was lying on one of the sofas, and as he turned his eyes he saw the face of Porculina staring intently and anxiously at him out of the candlelit darkness. After a moment, he realized that she was sitting on the edge of a marble-topped coffee table where he often liked to play jacks.

"Oh, hullo, Piggles," he said cheerfully, "what are you doing?"

"Oh, Gor-Gor," she answered in a somewhat dramatic and gushing voice, leaning forward and placing a cool trotter on his brow, "are you all right?"

"I think so," said Gorilla. And, indeed, he was aware of no particular discomfort in any part of his body. "Why shouldn't I be?"

The little pig sat up straight again. "Because that brute — that wicked miscreant who cannot flee the swift wings of justice, but who imagines he can, more fool he! — rendered you unconscious with an absolutely dastardly blow to your poor little apey head. He just conked you and just left you there in the snow, not even caring whether your stuffing got soaked or anything. The monster!"

Gorilla thought about this for a moment, then gingerly sat up, adjusted his nightcap, and said, "Yes, I remember that, more or less. He didn't really conk me, though. It was more of a *thonk* — a distinct *thonk*."

"Why, that's even worse!" Porculina cried. "The villain! The fiend!"

"Is it?" asked Gorilla. "Why?"

"Well..." Porculina looked a bit uncertain. "Well, it sounds worse to me. A *thonk*, forsooth! It sounds so... well, so... dreadful and pitiless.

Thonk. There, see what I mean? Just listen: *thonk*!"

"It was a quiet *thonk*," Gorilla remarked.

"That doesn't excuse him. Not at all. A *thonk* is a *thonk* in my book."

Gorilla looked around him. "Where's everyone else?"

"They've rejoined the chase," Porculina said. "I'd be with them too, but I simply couldn't leave you, not knowing how gravely that brigand may have hurt you. Teddy offered to stay, but I insisted he go. As the only trained detective among us, he has to be in on the hunt. Just so long as he remembers that when we catch the thief I'm the one who gets to say . . ." But she paused, lowered her eyes, and shook her head. "And, anyway, I'm afraid it's my fault the scoundrel got away. You see, I left my post." She looked up again, staring into Gorilla's eyes with an expression of sad earnestness. "It's just that, when I heard you cry out in searing agony like that, with that horrible soul-rending scream, I just couldn't help myself. I went running wildly through the snow in the direction the cry came from, calling your name, and having a terrible time finding my way through the maze. Teddy was calling out too, and Woof and Rolandus, but you didn't say a word, and we were all absolutely frantic — *frantic* — with worry. It seemed to take forever for us to find one another, and we never would have if Rolandus hadn't been able to shout instructions to me when I found myself lost, and then we all had to find you, and then to carry you out of the maze. And on the way out we saw that there were new tracks, and that felon — that beast without an ounce of pity in his miserable soul — had got away while we were looking for you. His tracks went off towards the front gate, but we couldn't follow them till we had got you back here and made sure you were all right. Rolandus and Woof went running back immediately and Teddy joined them about five minutes after. But I just had to stay and look after you, I was so worried."

"That was jolly nice of you," said Gorilla. "I'd have been terribly confused if you hadn't been here to explain things to me. I had a delightful little nap, though. I even had a dream of some kind — something about marshmallows . . . and baby bunnies . . ."

"Oh, but that terrifying cry of anguish you uttered!" Porculina said, wringing her trotters.

"You mean my 'ouch'? Yes, I thought it was rather fine," Gorilla said with an audible note of pride. "I put some real force into it, didn't I?"

"I almost came the first time you cried out, but then I heard what you told Teddy."

"Oh, you mean when I ran into that first statue?" said Gorilla. "Yes, that was silly of me. I've seen old Harold a thousand times before, and he's always in the same place . . . or I think he is. Anyway, I needn't have jumped at good old Harold Ironpaws — one of the greatest heroes in MacGorilla lore, you know . . . from the partly English branch of the clan."

"Is he?" said Porculina, not really paying full attention, but looking around her in a way that suggested she was growing impatient at the prolonged absence of the others. "What did he do?"

"It was magnificent!" Gorilla replied, clearly not discouraged by her preoccupied manner. "That statue commemorates a great day, an absolutely illustrated day, when he took sword in hand and charged on his own into the ranks of a great army of mighty marauders who had encircled the west wing of the castle and were advancing as a single front against its defenses. Or, at any rate, that's what he thought was happening. Actually, being a little shortsighted, he'd mistaken the rose bushes bordering the west lawn for an army of marauders, and so when he went charging out he ran into a particularly large bush covered with red roses. But it was a heroic charge, really truly, and it lives on in clan legend to this day as the most stirring episode in our whole grand history."

Gorilla's story had clearly captivated Porculina. Now, rather than glancing around distractedly, she was looking at him with wide eyes. "Yes, it must be," she said. "I can just picture it. How romantic! This was back in the early Middle Ages, was it?"

"No," said Gorilla with a small shake of his head, "just three years ago. Harold's my cousin and he was visiting for the week, on his way back to the Channel Isles, to Jersey where he lives — as so many toy gorillas do, you know. If he had remembered to wear his spectacles that morning, it probably would never have happened. But, as it was, he took one look out at the lawn after breakfast, cried, 'I say, Marauders!' and ran into my room to fetch a toy sword, and then charged across the sward into the ranks of the enemy bushes bellowing the clan's battle-cry, 'For MacGorilla and King or Queen Whoever It Is!' It really was glorious."

"I'll say it was," replied Porculina, releasing the breath she had been holding in her excitement. "He must be a very dashing fellow."

"Oh, yes," said Gorilla, "he's always dashing about everywhere. He's quite a world traveler, in fact, and he's always sending me postcards from some place or another. He just sent me one from Sumatra last week. Anyway, when word got around about his heroic charge, the whole clan decided to commission a statue here at the family seat."

"Imagine," said Porculina dreamily, obviously trying to summon up the picture of that famous day in her mind.

Just then, however, a light shone out in the adjoining foyer, there was the sound of steps, and Gorilla and Porculina turned to see someone approaching with the beam of a flashlight guiding the way.

"Who's there?" Porculina called out.

"Only me," Teddy's voice replied, and a moment later the little bear came into the sitting room, turned off his flashlight, and sat down in the armchair nearest his two friends and beside a small end table upon which a candle was burning. "We've lost him for now. But I'm afraid he hasn't necessarily lost us."

"What do you mean?" asked the pig.

"Well . . ." Teddy shook his head. "We tracked the thief out again, and his footprints led out to the guardhouse not far from the front gate, and from there to the fence. But clearly he couldn't get out, because the tracks turned back towards the castle and then . . . well, then they disappeared, just around the east wing, where he managed to shake snow down over his tracks from a tall bush near the wall. And then there was no other sign of him. So, for all we can tell, he's still on grounds or . . ." Teddy paused for a moment, looking at each of his friends gravely. "It may be that he's in the castle. There may have been another hidden door . . ."

Porculina gasped. Gorilla merely looked curious.

"Rolandus and Woof will keep watch for the remainder of the night," Teddy continued, "so we can get some sleep. In the morning we'll relieve them and . . ." Again he paused, and this time he seemed lost in thought.

"What?" Porculina prompted him.

"You see," the bear said, in a reluctant tone, "this was still too big a job for one thief. So there must be at least one accomplice around, and maybe more. And, since the tracks led back here . . . well, we have to face the possibility that one or more of your guests or staff may have been involved."

Porculina gasped again. Then she clapped her trotters together. "This really is a mystery novel!" she squealed.

"Oh, that's all right, then," said Gorilla. "If one of my guests or staff was involved, it was probably all just an understandable mistake. I make them all the time myself. We'll just wait till breakfast and ask everyone about it, and whoever it is will tell us what happened."

Porculina smirked. "Really, Gor-Gor," she said, "don't be silly. That'll never work."

"No," said Teddy quietly, "Gorilla's quite right. That's precisely what we should do."

CHAPTER 6
Pandas in the Kitchen

TEDDY WAS AWAKENED FROM A DEEP BUT BRIEF and not very refreshing sleep by a knocking at his door. He had asked Rolandus to rouse him early, so that he could begin his investigation and the two dogs could get some sleep. "Yes, yes," he called out groggily, "I'm up."

The door opened and Rolandus entered. "I'm sorry to wake you, sir, but breakfast will be in an hour and I believe you wished to get an early start. And, frankly, I can scarcely keep my eyes open."

"Yes, thanks," said Teddy, sitting up, rubbing his eyes, and then resting his head on his paws. "What a night. Any more news?"

"Well," said the dog, pausing to yawn behind a politely raised paw, "Woof and I made another reconnaissance of the grounds after dawn and for the life of us we can't see how the treasure could have been removed from the estate. The snow would show us if it had. And we can't find any trace of any robber in the castle itself. It's a large building, I admit, but we were very thorough indeed. I can't say with absolute certainty, but . . ." He shrugged wearily.

"To be honest," said the bear, drawing back his covers and swinging his feet over the edge of the bed, "I never thought the treasure left the premises." He stood up, smoothing his blue silk pajamas as he did so. "Our thief plainly knows a thing or two about this place, and if there's one secret passage there may be more, either in the castle or on the grounds. I don't doubt the whole hoard is concealed somewhere nearby. I don't suppose we have phones up, do we?"

"No, sir," Rolandus replied, "and the roads are still impassable. We won't be able to get the police up here today, I fear."

"So it's up to us," the little bear said grimly.

"Up to you, I'm afraid, sir. We shall have to rely on your expertise."

"And Blue," said Teddy, "how's he?"

"I just looked in on him," the dog replied, "and advised him to stay in bed for the remainder of the morning. I'll have Panda bring him some breakfast."

Teddy nodded. "Are Gorilla and Porculina up yet?" he asked.

"I'm just going to wake them now," said the dog.

"Well, then, I'll get changed and meet them downstairs. I'll have to interrogate all the staff and guests I'm afraid."

The dog raised an eyebrow and then cleared his throat. "Is that, ah, strictly necessary, sir?"

"Yes, I'm afraid so," said Teddy in a tone of regret. "We can't afford to overlook any clue. I know you don't want the hospitality of the castle to fall into disrepute, but ... " He raised his paws, palms upward, in a gesture of helplessness. "We simply must."

"Well, apart from myself," Rolandus said after a moment, "the whole staff at the moment is the maid Panda and her brother-in-law Pandus, our chef. Oh, and Panda's little son Pandulus — nice little chap — is around, and he likes to help out. They'll all be down in the kitchen getting breakfast ready."

"That's where I'll begin," said Teddy. "You should sleep, though. I'll ask Gorilla to show me the way. Or — well, I mean, Gorilla does know how to find the way to the kitchen, doesn't he?"

"On most occasions," said Rolandus.

*   *   *

When Teddy had brushed his teeth, changed from his pajamas into his bright red bowtie, and run a brush over his head, he made his way downstairs to the foyer. To his slight surprise, Gorilla and Porculina were both already below waiting for him. They always had been eager sorts, Teddy reflected, but, then again, that's the nature of toy pigs and toy gorillas; teddy bears are of a calmer, more contemplative cast of mind.

Porculina was in her little emerald-green beret again, while Gorilla's head was extravagantly wrapped in broad white bandages.

"Goodness, old fellow," said the little bear as he reached the bottom of the stairs, "you must have been hurt worse than we realized."

"What, this?" asked Gorilla with a cheerful laugh, slapping the side of his head. "No, but I thought I should wear it just the same. Porculina said it would let the world know ... " He paused. "What was that again, Piggles? Let the world know ... "

"Let the world know," said Porculina fiercely, "how viciously you were attacked by that monster last night, and what a desperate villain he is, and how he will cringe like the craven beast he is when at last he's run to earth in his lair and exposed to the clear unwavering light of pure justice, which he foolishly thinks he can flee, but which is swifter than the wind. And, anyway," she added, reaching up and neatly tucking the end of one of the bandages in, "you look absolutely darling like that. It's just like a wonderful turban, and you look just like a mighty Persian king."

"Do I really?" asked Gorilla, plainly delighted. "Have you a mirror on you?"

"Old fellow," said Teddy, "before looking in a mirror, could you take me down to the kitchens? I thought I should start . . ."

"Yes, we know," Porculina interrupted. "Roly told us everything. Off we go, then. The investigation begins. I suppose I'll have to be the slightly slow-witted sidekick detective whom you'll ask baffling questions I can't answer, just so you can supply the right answers, and I'll have to say things like 'By George, my dear old bear, I hadn't thought of that,' or 'Brilliant, my dear old Teddy, why couldn't I see that?' That's how it goes, isn't it?"

"Yes," said Teddy, "that's an absolutely indispensable job. Thanks, I'll be grateful for your help. So, old fellow, the kitchens?"

"I just adore kitchens," Porculina remarked.

"Let's go then," said Gorilla heartily, "there are stairs down to the kitchens just around . . ." He began to point to the right side of the large central stairwell, then thought better of it and pointed to the left, then thought better of that and pointed back to the right. "Yes, just around there. Follow me."

Porculina immediately fell in at Gorilla's side and the two began striding off in the direction Gorilla had indicated, swinging their arms happily. Teddy waited a moment with a raised eyebrow, and then followed a few paces behind.

"Can you guess how my cousin Harold got the nickname Ironpaws, by any chance?" Gorilla was asking Porculina.

"No," said the little pig in a genuinely interested voice, "I can't."

"It's because he was so enormously strong. Even as a little ape, he could crush a whole grape in one of his paws. Imagine that — just absolutely crush it!"

After a momentary pause, Porculina said, "But Gor-Gor, can't anyone crush a grape?"

Gorilla said nothing to this for several seconds. Then, halting for a moment and turning to the little pig with a deeply deliberative look in his eyes, he said, "You know, that's never occurred to me. Are you sure? I suppose — well, I suppose I'll just have to try for myself the next time I have a grape in hand." He pursed his lips and said "Hmm" to himself, as if considering the matter at a very deep level, and then resumed walking.

*   *   *

They were heading in the wrong direction of course, but after only fifteen minutes or so of going around corners, down one flight of stairs and up two, coming to the door of Gorilla's bedroom, and then setting off again, they finally righted their course, aided at the last by Porculina, who suddenly shouted, "I smell food!" just as they were passing the door leading to the right set of stairs. A few moments later the three friends entered the large main kitchen, with its long central work table set in the middle of a bright and immaculate white floor, and its racks of gleaming copper pots and pans hanging from the ceiling, and its immense ovens filling the room with a delightful warmth. The pretty maid Panda was there, standing over a large silver salver heaped with crisp Belgian waffles and golden pancakes and gleaming blackberries; the air was fragrant with honey and melting butter and bananas and baking bread and any number of other delicious aromas.

"Oh, sir — sirs, miss," Panda said in a startled voice, wiping her paws on her red striped apron, "this is quite a surprise. I hope breakfast isn't late — chef will be back in a moment and I'll bring everything up promptly."

"We're not here about breakfast," said Teddy, "though it all smells wonderful. We're here because of the events of last night. I suppose Rolandus told you?"

"Oh, yes," she said in a tone of deep dismay, "isn't it dreadful! Oh, sir," — she came towards Gorilla — "your poor head!"

Gorilla smiled. "Yes, it's rather splendid, isn't it? Just like a Persian cat, Porculina tells me."

"We just need to ask a few questions," said Teddy, "and then we'll be out of the way."

"Questions about what?" a deep, rather gruff voice said from the far corner of the kitchen.

Teddy turned to see that two other toy pandas had entered from a door to the right at the far end of the kitchen. One was quite a little fellow carrying a can of golden syrup in one hand and a blue bowl of slivered almonds in the other. The other, however — the one who had spoken — was a fully grown male panda wearing a tall chef's toque on his head, a chef's white double-breasted tunic around his ample middle, and a chef's checkered trousers, and he was carrying a large oval platter covered with slices of banana and plantain.

"Hullo, Pandus," called Gorilla happily, "and hello there, little Pandulus, old chap."

"Good morning, milord," said Pandus; then, curtly nodding to the other two, he added, "Good morning, miss, good morning, sir."

"Good morning," Pandulus chimed in merrily.

"This is our resident genius," said Gorilla, "the finest chef . . . well, in the universe, I think. Or maybe in Scotland. One or the other."

"Oh, strawberries, I'm such an admirer of your work!" Porculina suddenly said in a high effusive voice. "I've been just — just *enraptured* since my very first bite of your . . . your masterpieces!"

"Thank you, milord," the large Panda said with a somewhat embarrassed frown, "and thank you, miss." Then he walked to the central work table, set down the platter he was carrying, gestured for the little panda to come along and set the syrup and honey down as well, and then turned again to the three visitors to his kitchen. "I believe I heard you saying you had to ask some questions."

"Yes," said Teddy with a nod, "some very important questions, but nothing that should take too . . ."

"Let me handle this," Gorilla suddenly interrupted. "I know just what to do."

"But, um, Gorilla . . ." Teddy began.

But Gorilla turned to the chef and, raising an emphatic finger in the air before him, said, "Listen, old fellow, this is absolutely vital. Think carefully. Have you any grapes in the kitchen here?"

Pandus was silent for several seconds, staring blankly at Gorilla, as if taken entirely off guard. Then, finally, he said, "No, sir, I'm afraid we haven't just now. Is that . . . is that all?"

Gorilla looked down at his feet, scratched his ear, then shook his head. "I certainly can't think of anything else right now." He raised his eyes again. "Well, I suppose we should go up for breakfast, then."

"Wait," said Teddy, "there are actually just a *few* more questions. You know," — he looked meaningfully at Gorilla — "the treasure . . . the robbery."

"Oh, yes," said Gorilla, "*that*. Well, if you think it's important."

"I do," said Teddy. Then he turned to Pandus and Panda, who were now standing a few feet apart. "You both know of the robbery last night?"

"Yes," said Pandus. "I'm sorry to see that your injury was so . . . grave, milord," he added, looking at Gorilla with a worried expression.

"Doesn't hurt a bit," said Gorilla, knocking himself three times on the top of his head with his fist. "Quite a striking piece of headgear, though, isn't it?"

"Yes, milord. Very."

"The first thing we need to know," Teddy continued, "is where all of you were when the theft occurred."

"Oh, my," Panda suddenly gasped, "you don't — you don't suspect us, sir, do you?"

"Not at all," said Teddy, waving his paws in the air, "I suspect no one yet, but I need to gather all the facts I can. I'm afraid that, until we have some way of getting through to the police and they have some way of getting through to us, I have to conduct the investigation according to standard procedure."

"Well," Pandus said, "yes, as you say. We are a bit pressed for time here, sir, so if you'll just tell us what you need to know." His tone was polite, but with perhaps just a hint of surliness in it. "Without any electricity, everything is a bit more difficult."

Suddenly, and quite surprisingly, Porculina cleared her throat, strode forward, thrust her trotter out accusingly at Pandus, and said, in an alarmingly savage voice, "What we need to know, my good fellow, is whether you and your sister-in-law here are the dastardly villains who plundered this estate last night, brutally assaulted this noble gorilla, and now foolishly imagine you can flee the swift wings of avenging justice! Speak up, if you dare!" Then, just as suddenly, she took a step back and, in her normal sweet voice, said, "Muffins, I hope that didn't sound rude. It's just that I'm playing the role of the slow-witted sidekick detective and its part of my job to jump to unwarranted conclusions and to behave stupidly at awkward moments."

"Strictly speaking," said Teddy mildly, "that's not really necessary. Not just yet, at any rate. But" — he patted her gently on the shoulder — "that was extremely impressive, old girl. You had me quaking." And he truly was impressed.

Pandus said nothing, a quizzical expression on his face, but Panda turned to her son and said, "Off you go, dear, set the table for our breakfast in the staff dining room, please."

"Right, mum," the little panda replied, obviously not at all bothered by any of this, and dashed off across the length of the kitchen and out through another door beyond the ovens.

"I do wish you'd all just come and eat with the rest of us," said Gorilla, "the way we normally do. I don't see why you need to use that silly staff dining room."

Pandus began to stir, clasping his paws before him, looking quickly over his shoulder at the platters of food, and then saying, now with a clear note of impatience in his voice, "It's only that, with so many guests, we take a certain pride in doing things properly. Panda," he said suddenly, turning to the maid, "please put the cover on that salver before the food gets cold."

"Oh, yes," said Panda, whose mind had obviously been elsewhere for a moment, and she hurried to comply.

"And then please see that the banana porridge isn't burning," he added, pointing to a large pot placidly steaming away atop the range of the middle oven, a bright blue flame flickering beneath it. Then he turned back to Teddy. "We'll tell you anything we can, sir, but we really must get back to work."

"Right, I understand," said Teddy. "Well, the questions are simple enough. I suppose you were all in bed at the time of the robbery, anyway."

"No," Panda called from the oven, where she was now stirring the porridge with a large wooden spoon, "only Pandulus was asleep. I was sitting in here, over there" — she pointed to a corner where two simple chairs were set beside a small round table — "snacking on bamboo shoots. We keep a huge store of them in the back — it's our favorite food, you know. Anyway, we'd been up late, what with the loss of electricity and making sandwiches and such. And then I couldn't sleep, and I always get a little hungry when I can't sleep."

"Don't we all!" said Porculina with deep feeling.

"Were you here too?" Teddy asked Pandus.

"Yes," the chef replied, "or, rather, no, not precisely. I was back that way" — he pointed towards the door through which he had entered the kitchen a few moments earlier — "through there, in the pantry and the larder, taking stock."

"I find larders and pantries absolutely fascinating," Porculina remarked.

Teddy nodded thoughtfully. "Do you often take stock so very late at night?" he asked.

"No, sir," said Pandus, "but when I realized we had been cut off by all this snow and that we wouldn't be getting any deliveries from town for perhaps a few days, and that we had so many guests to provide for, I became rather worried about how we could go about rearranging the menus I had planned for today and tomorrow . . ."

Porculina suddenly gave a small squeal of alarm. The others turned to her and saw that she was staring at the chef with wide, horrified eyes, and that she was visibly trembling. "You're not saying," she said in a strangely weak and quavering voice, "I mean, you're not implying . . . you don't think . . ." She closed her eyes now, as if trying to summon up the courage to say it. "You don't think we might . . . run out of food, do you?"

Pandus breathed in deeply, as if relieved. "No, miss, no fear of that. We have plenty of supplies. Our ovens use gas or wood, and we have several old-fashioned iceboxes, so nothing will spoil. The question was one of preparing a menu with the ingredients at hand, without disgracing ourselves by serving something inferior."

"Oh," Porculina said, releasing her breath slowly, opening her eyes, and smiling like someone who had just received a reprieve from a terrible fate, "for a moment I feared the very worst."

"Never worry, old girl," Gorilla said encouragingly, "why, we have a whole hothouse full of ripe bananas around back."

"Yes," said Pandus with a weary nod, "that we do. Is there anything else, sir?"

"You both saw each other?" Teddy asked.

Panda had now returned from her station by the porridge. "Yes, of course," she said. "Pandus saw me when he went through the kitchen, and I saw him go into the back."

"And how long was he there?" Teddy persisted.

"Quite some time," Panda replied. "But there's only one way in and out and I never left my chair while he was back there, so I knew that he was in there all the while."

"It did take some time," Pandus added. "I had to rethink all the meals for today and tomorrow, and I had only a few candles lit back there. But, as Panda says, she was here when I went in and when I went out."

"How long, would you say?" asked Teddy.

"Half an hour," said Pandus after a moment's consideration.

"Maybe forty-five minutes," said Panda.

"And you both heard the loud crash from upstairs?" Teddy asked.

"Well, yes," said Panda, "but it wasn't all that loud down here. I mean, it was loud, but I thought someone had just knocked something over in the dark overhead, or that Blue and Woof were still working on the auxiliary generator, which is just around the corner and down another level from here, and that they were banging on something. It made me jump — don't get me wrong — but it wasn't shockingly loud."

"Scarcely audible at all in the back," Pandus said. "I think I heard something, but I didn't think any more of it than Panda did. Really, though, we must be getting breakfast ready. With Rolandus having gone to rest, I'll have to help carry things up to the breakfast parlor." Now his voice had a touch of urgency in it, and perhaps a dash of ire.

"Right," said Teddy, "of course." Then, looking towards the door to the back kitchen, he said, "Can I just have a look at the pantry and larder, just so I can get a picture in my head of where everyone was? It might help me figure out just how the sound traveled from above, and what caused all the noise."

Pandus was clearly displeased by the further waste of time, but he agreed to show Teddy the back rooms. Porculina insisted on coming, since she could never resist any exploration of any larder. The door led into a smaller kitchen with a single stove and a few work surfaces and sinks, at whose far end was another door leading into a small corridor that opened onto a pantry on the right and a larder to the left. Both were quite ordinary and quite well stocked. The larder had high sturdy sets of open metal shelves, absolutely filled with vast reserves of foods — fruits and cheeses and jams and butter and flour and so on and so on — and at the far end were several large crates brimming over with bananas and, in a small alcove to one side of the far end, a great garner full of bamboo shoots. Teddy said he had seen enough after only three minutes or so, but it took some effort to convince Porculina that they should leave.

"It's like a magical kingdom in here," she said quietly. "One could get lost in its enchantment."

"Breakfast is waiting," Teddy finally said.

This woke her from her reverie. "Yes, yes, of course."

The three of them returned to the kitchen, and Teddy, Porculina, and Gorilla began to leave. But, just at the door, Teddy turned around. "Excuse me, one last question," he said.

Pandus, who had returned to the platter he had brought into the kitchen, heaved a sigh of frustration. "Yes, sir?"

"The two of you," Teddy said, "you're both quite happy with your jobs?"

"Oh, quite!" said Panda as she turned off the heat under the porridge. "This is the best situation I've ever had, and Laird MacGorilla is a wonderful employer."

"I really am," Gorilla observed earnestly.

"And you, Chef?" Teddy said.

Pandus approached a few steps and then shrugged. "Yes, I suppose I am. It's a very good situation, as Panda says."

"But I understand you'd like to open a restaurant someday."

Pandus nodded. "Well, yes, we all have our aspirations. One likes to set up in business for oneself. It's just a dream for now, but one day I'd like to do it. It would give me a freer hand, and more range to work with."

"Range?" said Teddy.

"Well, yes," Pandus replied. "I mean, here" — he held out his paws, as if indicating everything around him — "there's plenty to do, of course. But it's a limited cuisine. I'd like to explore all sorts of other cuisines, especially cuisines centered on bamboo. Bamboo's quite succulent, you know, if cooked properly. Here, though, everything is bananas. Bananas all the time, every day, every night. It's challenging and rewarding, I know, but — well, there's more to life than just bananas."

Gorilla let out a gasp, stared with widening eyes, and then walked over to the chef and took him by the shoulders. "My dear old bear," he said in a strained and anxious voice, "think what you're saying." He gave Pandus a few gentle shakes. "Pull yourself together. You're letting the stress get to you. You sound like a lunatic." Then, looking back over his shoulder at Teddy, he said, "Pay him no mind. He's tired and all the events of last night have clearly rattled his nerves."

Pandus bowed his head. "Yes, milord," he said, "of course you're right. It's all been a bit taxing." Then, gently extracting himself from Gorilla's clasp, he added, "But we must be getting things ready."

"Good," said Gorilla. "You had me worried. Listen, why don't you let me carry some of these things up to the breakfast room?"

A look of alarm appeared on the faces of both pandas, and they courteously but decisively moved to interpose themselves between Gorilla and the food.

"Oh, no, sir," said Panda in an alarmed voice, "that would ... that would never do. It would be, well ... improper."

"Yes," Pandus concurred, with a note of agitation, "perfectly improper. We'll take care of it, milord. Thank you, but ..."

"Stuff and nonsense!" Gorilla cried. "I don't stand on formality of that sort, as you well know. Anyway, everyone knows we're shorthanded here. We all have to pitch in. I'll just take that dish ..."

"Honestly, milord," Pandus persisted, his tone becoming desperate, "we couldn't allow ... we'd feel ashamed ... we ... really ..."

Teddy, however, had grasped the problem and quickly interjected, "Gorilla, old fellow, I think you ought to show us to the breakfast room and leave all of that in the capable paws of these good pandas. You may want to show us a thing or two on the way ... and I'd love to hear the tale of your cousin ... what did you call him? Ironpaws?"

"Really?" said Gorilla turning to his friend with a gleeful smile. "Well, it is a stirring tale."

"Indeed, it is," said Porculina eagerly, also delighted by Teddy's request, "and I'd love to hear it again. Oh, but do let's go. I'm famished."

CHAPTER 7

Interrogations Over Waffles

THE BREAKFAST ROOM WAS A DELIGHTFUL OPEN space, obviously built as an annex to the mediaeval structure sometime in the nineteenth century, and full of all the natural light that the older portions of the castle totally excluded. It was a sort of large enclosed portico, its many huge French doors and windows affording a generous view of the south grounds (now blanketed by snow) and a small ornamental lake. Corinthian columns rose from a broad gleaming marble floor and supported a high, vaulted Victorian ceiling with a lovely large circular dome of pale blue glass at its center. There were small, elegant wrought-iron breakfast tables, painted white, with equally elegant wrought-iron chairs arranged about them, and tall broad-leaved tropical plants rose from large marble planters on all sides, and the long mahogany and marble buffet standing to one side was covered with steaming platters and carafes. The buffet also held stacks of glistening porcelain service adorned with images of Gorillas, bananas, and whistles. Everything was washed in a fresh, bright, wintry light. Not long after Teddy, Gorilla, and Porculina had seated themselves around a single table, the five guests who had not yet heard about the robbery arrived, and soon after that more marvelously fragrant dishes began appearing from the kitchens, carried up in several trips by a cheerful Panda and a somewhat sullen Pandus.

Gorilla went about greeting everyone happily and apologizing that the food was a bit late and promising to explain the bandage on his head later and asking whether it made him look like a Persian carpet. Then, when everyone had served himself or herself from the buffet and taken a seat, Teddy stood up from the table at the farthest remove from the food, where he was sitting with Porculina and Gorilla, walked to the buffet, turned, and clearly but politely asked for everyone's attention. Everyone except Porculina — who was far too engrossed in finishing off her third Belgian waffle to pay him much attention — fell silent and looked at the little bear. In as few words as possible, and in a very calm tone, Teddy narrated the events of the previous night. There were, of course, gasps of alarm and exclamations of outrage, not to mention a few calls for the police, and at once everyone began speaking loudly and excitedly — everyone, that is, but Cuttles, who merely sat by himself at one of the remoter tables gazing despondently at his plate of dry toast and idly fiddling with his bright crimson cravat.

When Teddy had brought the room to order again, and reminded everyone that the police could not be reached as yet, and said that he would be conducting the investigation for now, he added, "I shall need to ask some questions of you all — just to see if you can help me piece together the sequence of events, or provide me with any clues. Normally, I'd speak to each of you in private, but our resources are limited, and we're somewhat pressed for time if the robbers are, as I suspect, still in the vicinity . . ."

This too elicited a chorus of gasps, squeaks, squawks, and croaks from the guests, and Teddy was obliged to call for quiet again.

"You don't mean to say," asked Miss Raccoon, who was sharing a table with Mr MacAw, "that you think that these desperate criminals might still be on the premises?"

"It's a distinct possibility," Teddy admitted, and again had to raise his hands and his voice to bring quiet to the room. "Please, I beg all of you, let's try to keep calm. We're all together here, and we'll try to remain together if we can, so we're really quite safe. It's just that . . ."

"Excuse me," Mr MacAw suddenly said, "but, just out of curiosity, the items stolen didn't happen to include those . . . those lovely bagpipes of our host's, did they?"

"Not at all!" Gorilla called out loudly, peering over the enormous stack of banana pancakes on his plate and over the still higher stack of waffles on Porculina's. "Not to worry. They're quite untouched."

"Oh," said the parrot quietly. "I'm very . . . relieved."

"As I was saying," Teddy continued, "as time is of the essence, I should like simply to ask all of you a few questions while we're all assembled . . ."

But now Cuttles spoke up, in a somber but emphatic voice: "I too am relieved. I thought last night's music one of the most truly moving experiences I've had in a very long time indeed."

Now the room fell perfectly silent. Even Teddy had momentarily forgotten what he was going to say.

"Ye, um," Ribbit at last said, "ye truly liked it, did ye? I mean, didna we all, o' course, but . . . weel . . ."

"I was entranced," the squid replied with obvious sincerity. "The melodies were so very hauntingly sad — so bruisingly beautiful, if I may say."

"I'm so pleased you liked them," Gorilla said, standing on his chair to see better over his pancakes (Porculina's waffles were now all but gone) and smiling proudly. "To hear that from so distinguished an artist warms my heart. But, you know, the melodies weren't really supposed to be sad. They're dance tunes."

"Ah," said Cuttles with a tolerant smile, waving a tentacle nonchalantly, "all melodies are sad — if you only know how to listen. Sorrow is the inner essence of all beauty. Your music... well, it seemed to reach right down into my soul, and just to... to *wrench* something out of me."

"Yes," said Miss Raccoon in a thoughtful tone, "I suppose I might put it that way myself."

Gorilla was clearly overwhelmed. "You know, I only just learned to play last week," he said.

"One of them was so shatteringly evocative," the squid continued. "It put me in mind of that long monologue from the thirty-second act of my latest play, the one spoken by the young oyster who loses his ball. You may recall the one I mean, Gorilla." And here he began declaiming, in a rich, vibrant, almost velvety baritone that sounded as though it were just at the edge of tears:

> "Ah, woe! Ah, topmost woe! Thus have I had
> Joy's cup — e'en as I fain would quaff — now dashed
> So cruelly from my trembling..."

Teddy, however, had recovered himself, and this time he did the interrupting: "Please, everyone, this is truly vital. All I want to do is to ask each of you whether you heard or saw anything last night that could help us. And, of course," — he assumed an apologetic expression — "I'm afraid I'll have to ask you all to account for your own whereabouts... and whether you can corroborate your story. And please," — he raised his paws over his head to prevent the outburst of voices he feared — "don't think I'm implying anything, or accusing anyone here. It's really just a matter of standard procedure."

"Well!" said Mr MacAw indignantly, but nothing more.

"You don't suspect us, do you?" asked Miss Raccoon, with a winsome flutter of her long eyelashes. "I'd be just mortified if I thought you thought..."

"Oh, of course not," Teddy said hastily, and it almost appeared as if he was beginning to blush. "I would never suspect you, Miss Racooning — Miss Raccoon, rather. I could never . . ." He looked about him at the faces of all the guests. "Or any of you, of course. I simply must ask. So, if I may, I'll just — oh, Pigsy, watch out!"

"Sorry," the little pig said as she bustled past him towards the buffet, "didn't mean to step on your toes. Just going for seconds."

Teddy dropped his head and waited until Porculina had filled her plate again and returned to her seat, gracefully balancing the tottering tower of waffles, pancakes, buttered toast, and berries as she did so.

"All right," said the bear, "if we're all settled, I'll just go around the room, and ask each of you a few simple questions. Now, Alasdair, I'll start with you."

"Please," said the parrot, crossing his wings peevishly, "feel free to call me Mr MacAw."

Teddy shrugged. "Very well, Mr MacAw, were you awake when the noise that roused so many of us from our beds was heard?"

"I think not," answered the parrot, staring haughtily away into empty space. "I admit that it was some time before I quite recovered from — or, rather, quite overcame my excitement at the . . . stirring music of the night's entertainments. But, at the time of last night's incident, at least if I understand the timeline you have presented, I was quite asleep. As for whether I can confirm my alibi — which is, let's be honest, what you're asking me to confirm — I fear not, as I'm not in the habit of sleeping in public."

"Please, Mr MacAw," said Teddy imploringly, "don't lose your temper. This is a matter of simple procedure. I'm trying to construct a narrative — that's all."

The parrot partially relented; at least he deigned to look at Teddy before uttering a quiet "Harrumph!"

"Weel, we can corroborate his tale," Ribbit interjected from the table he was sharing with his nephew in the center of the floor. "As it happens, neither I nor the wee taddie here could fall asleep fer some time. Who could sleep after that . . . heroic performance by the Laird? So we were sitting up playing draughts — or checkers, as ye might call it. And we're roomed reet next to Mr MacAw, and — not to put too fine a point on it — we heard him snorin' . . . quite loudly."

Mr MacAw now looked even more indignant. "Snoring?" he asked with wide eyes. "Parrots do not . . . *snore*."

"Aye, that's true enough," said Ribbit. "It's not quite a snore. Parrots seem to make a very distinctive sort of noise when they're asleep. Something between a snore and a squawk."

"A squork," Jumping Bean helpfully suggested. "I can try to imitate it if you like."

"That won't be necessary," said Teddy.

"It certainly won't!" said Mr MacAw, ruffling his wings violently.

"Anyway," Teddy continued, "that establishes Mr MacAw's whereabouts. But, Mr Ribbit, did you hear the crash?"

"Aye," said Ribbit, "we certainly heard soomaught, but at the back o' the castle, behind all those big doors, it wasn't quite as loud as you make it oot. Where we were, it sounded like something had been knocked over in the dark — nothing to worry aboot. So we just played on."

"I won six of eight games," Jumping Bean remarked.

"We heard nae more, not even any of you lot moving about," Ribbit continued. "I suppose it was an hour later that we went to our beds again. We slept weel enough from there on."

Jumping Bean merely nodded and resumed eating his banana soufflé in caramel sauce.

"Well," said Teddy, "I suppose that's all I need to ask you. So, then, Mr MacCuttle — Cuttles, if I may — were you asleep or awake when the sound was heard?"

"Oh, quite awake," the squid replied sadly. "I usually am. The perfumed, dewy balm of sleep is rarely shaken down upon my weary eyes. I'm of a wakeful nature — so many things weigh on my mind. I was sitting up in bed at the time, listening to the stones around me aging."

"Ah," said Teddy. Then, after a moment, he added, "I wasn't aware one could hear that."

"Oh, but one can," Cuttles replied in a darkly ominous tone. "One can."

"Well, then, could you tell me what you heard, and whether you heard or saw anything else that might be pertinent to our investigation?"

"Apart from the stones aging," Cuttles said, "I heard — at the time you mention — a distant crash, or series of crashes, and then a great desolate chasm of resonant silence, which seemed somehow full of the music of . . . desolation, shall we say?"

"And did you go to investigate?" asked Teddy.

"No, why would I?" said the squid. "I assumed it was merely a tower at some end of the castle collapsing, as the result of some ancient ancestral curse, or the auxiliary generator exploding. Nothing that would have surprised me. Anyway, I rarely go walking about if I can avoid it. It isn't very easy getting about on one's fins or tentacles on dry land. I mean, if you want to know what's it's like, try walking on your fingertips and nose and lips sometime."

Teddy nodded. "I see what you mean."

"Don't misunderstand me — they're fine things for swimming about in the ocean, tentacles are," Cuttles continued. "They're absolutely capital in the ocean. Really, it's a pity I have such a loathing for water. I detest getting wet."

"And I suppose that, of course, there were no witnesses to your whereabouts just then?"

"None I know of," said Cuttles, "except, of course, the cold eye of fate."

"Well, then," Teddy began, but stopped as Porculina hastily trotted past him.

"Thirds," she called airily over her shoulder.

"Well," Teddy resumed once the little pig had returned to her seat, "I suppose that leaves only . . ." He turned to Miss Raccoon, and for a moment a shy and slightly idiotic grin appeared on his face. Then, clearing his throat and composing himself, he said, "Miss Raccooning . . ."

"Raquel, please," she said.

Teddy swallowed. "Thank you. Well, then — if it's not too much trouble — I mean, if you don't mind — can you tell us whether you were awake at the time in question?"

"Why yes, of course," the raccoon replied, her honeyed voice issuing from smiling lips, "I was wide awake. I too was far too . . . far too *excited* by that . . . absolutely divine music our host played for us last night."

"I think I hear a request for an encore," Gorilla remarked in a pleased voice.

For a moment the room seemed frozen. Only Cuttles moved; waving two tentacles before him grandly, he cried out, "How exquisite!"

"Can you," Teddy at last continued, "remember precisely where you were, and what you did, and whether you heard anything else . . . um, Raquel?"

Miss Raccoon fluttered her long eyelashes again and smiled even more attractively. "For you, Mr Bear, gladly. Or I suppose I should call you Teddy, since we're such good friends now. I was sitting in an armchair reading a fascinating magazine article about me in a very glamorous magazine, and admiring the lovely photographs, when I heard something loud — a bang or a bash or a clatter — but far away."

A happily dazed look had appeared on Teddy's features when Miss Raccoon had addressed him by his first name, and it was a moment or two before he could quite resume his calm professional expression. When he did, he asked, "And did you react? I mean, did you go to explore, or call out? And did you hear or see anything else after that?"

"I did indeed react," she answered. "I stood up from my chair and dropped my magazine. But, when I heard nothing more, I simply thought it was a servant running into something in the dark, or something like that, so I sat down and went on reading. I put out all but one of the candles and went to bed not long after that."

"And of course, there's no way of corroborating that," Teddy remarked casually, "but that's quite understandable."

"Oh, but there is," the raccoon said. "There was a witness."

"Who?" asked Teddy.

"Why, me," she replied. "When I stood up on hearing that noise, I happened to see myself distinctly reflected in the large mirror over the vanity table. So you see, not only was I in the room, I clearly *witnessed* myself in the room at just that crucial moment."

"Oh," said Teddy with a furrowed brow.

"Well, that proves it to me," said Gorilla, licking his spoon.

But Porculina raised her snout from her plate with a somewhat baffled look on her face. "I don't know about that," she said. "I mean . . . does that work? Can she corroborate her own story?"

"It's, ah, unusual," Teddy acknowledged.

"You see, Gor-Gor," the little pig continued, "she's herself, and so she's not really *another* witness as such — if you see what I mean."

"Oh, I know that," Gorilla replied with a dismissive wave of his hand. "You must think I'm terribly empty-headed. But don't you see? If she were lying about being in her room, and then she were lying about seeing herself in the mirror, why that would mean she'd have to lie *twice*, and no one would be so dishonest as all that."

Teddy looked at his friend affectionately and then sadly shook his head. "My dear old ape," he said, "you have such a good nature that you can't suspect evil in anybody. I'm sorry to have to tell you this, but in my years on the force I knew hardened criminals who were so shameless that they would lie as many as *three times*. In fact, I've often been brought in especially for cases like that, particularly when the suspect is a human being. It seems they have a very hard time lying to teddy bears — it makes them feel awful, because it reminds them of childhood and mother and things of that sort. I've seen grown men break down in tears and start calling me things like 'Mr Cuddles' or 'Bonbon,' and then pour out their souls to me. But, up until that point, they'll often go on lying till they can't go any further."

Gorilla stared at his friend emptily for several seconds. Then, as very rarely happened, a look of dismay, even of sorrow, appeared on his face. He bowed his little round head and wagged it slowly. "I never knew there was such wickedness in the world," he said quietly.

The room was silent for several seconds.

"Anyway," said Teddy at last, "that doesn't apply here." He smiled as charmingly as he could, if a little nervously, at the lovely raccoon. "We certainly don't suspect you of lying at all."

Still Gorilla sat motionless with his head hanging down, almost in an attitude of defeat.

"Cheer up, darling old apey," Porculina said. "Criminals can learn better ways. Look, I'm just going for my fourths. Wouldn't you like me to bring you a lovely bowl of cherries?"

"Oh, yes," Gorilla said, raising his head, suddenly cheerful again. "With plenty of banana slices mixed in, and cream poured over."

"All right, then," said Teddy, looking around at the other guests, "I think there's nothing else for now. I'm sorry to have troubled you with this nasty business, but we'll get to the bottom of it. So, if you'll excuse me, I'm quite hungry myself." He looked over his shoulder at the buffet, which was still plenteously heaped with all sorts of delectable things, despite Porculina's frequent raids upon it. "Thank you," he added.

Everyone except Mr MacAw nodded at him graciously.

*   *   *

A little while later, as he sat eating his bowlful of porridge, berries, bananas, and honey, and as all the other guests were talking among themselves or (in the case of Cuttles) sighing loudly at odd intervals and giving off occasional faint sprays of ink, Teddy told his friends that they must go back to the treasure room to resume the investigation.

"Oh, not yet," Gorilla protested. "I want to show you the castle first. There's so much to see and you haven't had any rest. Please, I insist you let me show you around."

"There's no time," the little bear replied. "Who knows where the thieves are hiding, or where they've stashed your treasure. A crucial moment lost . . . "

"Fiddle-faddle and bruised bananas!" Gorilla interrupted. "I won't hear of it. The curse will bring the treasure back one way or the other, but I have your company only for a few days. Oh, please please please! I especially want to take you to the fountain room. It's my favorite place in the whole estate, and it's very special in its design. It's under the hothouse. I mean, down on the ground floor. The hothouse is a wonderful conservatory, all of beautiful greeny glass, full of banana trees and other wonderful plants, and its floor is all iron trellis or tracery or whatever — you know, iron work with lots of leafy designs in it, but not absolutely solid, so one can see right down. And under it is another room that one goes down to by a spiral iron staircase, and that's the fountain room. And it was all my idea, and it's absolutely unbelievably wonderful."

"What's so special about it?" Porculina asked.

Gorilla tapped the side of his nose with one finger and winked. "You'll see, Piggles. Oh, please, you too, I have to show you."

Teddy took a deep breath. "All right," he said. "Anyway, with all this snow about, no one's going anywhere just yet."

And so, after Teddy had finished his second course and Porculina had bravely decided to forgo her eighth, Gorilla took his friends on a tour of the castle.

CHAPTER 8

All At Sea

"AVAST, MATEYS!" CRIED GORILLA, WAVING HIS wooden cutlass over his head with such vigor that he knocked the brim of his wide, plumed pirate's hat down over his eyes. "Unfurl the mains'l! Hard a-starboard! And tack hard a-port also, ye swabs! Open the scuttles! Scupper the ship! No! Wait! Belay that last order, Mr Pig!"

"Aye-aye, Cap'n!" hollered Porculina, pacing from one side of the boat to the other in her large pirate's boots and waving her cutlass with a flamboyance comparable to Gorilla's. "There's a red sky to lee," she added ominously.

"What's our speed, Mr Bear?" Gorilla cried; and, when he received no answer, he added, "Look lively, Mister, or I'll have ye keel-hauled! Ye'll be supper for the sharks!" He pointed to a few large goldfish swimming lazily around the prow.

"Oh, yes," said Teddy, adjusting his eye-patch and the red kerchief tied about his head. "I mean, aye-aye, Cap'n." He looked at the coiled and knotted rope slowly unwinding itself as it was drawn over the stern. "Um, say, half a knot, Cap'n . . . give or take a strand or two."

"Put on more sail!" Gorilla shouted to no one in particular. "We'll need a full press to catch that galleon, me hearties! And stay well off that lee shore there!" He pointed vaguely off to the left. "Don't lose her, Mr Roly!"

Rolandus — who was standing at the helm with his paws resting on the wheel, dressed in his butler's tail-coat, winged collar, and tie, but with an incongruous green velvet tricorne on his head — said, "As you wish, sir."

Gorilla turned to look at the dog with an expression of mild vexation on his face. "Oh, come on, Roly, please try to get into the spirit of the thing."

Rolandus shut his eyes for a moment and sighed. "Aye-aye . . . Cap'n," he said drily. "Though I might add . . . um, Cap'n, that were we to follow all your commands to the letter we would run aground or sink . . . Cap'n."

"That's the spirit!" Gorilla cried out happily. "But don't worry. I've always brought us safe to harbor in the past."

Teddy looked around admiringly. He was seated just behind Rolandus, at the rear of a vessel hardly bigger than a rowboat, though it was built to look like a deep-hulled pirate ship with a flat deck and lovely gold brightwork, and had two masts with broad square-rigged sails of white crêpe paper, tied off by kite string to the rails, and two little brass cannons mounted to the gunwales pointing off to either side of the bowsprit (which was shaped like a banana). Porculina was farther forward and Gorilla was standing in the bow. They were "sailing" in the immense fountain that Gorilla had had installed below ground level in the hothouse — though, in fact, the boat was propelled not by any breeze but by a small, quiet, battery-operated outboard engine. As Gorilla had said, the floor above was a network of open ironwork and catwalks, so the daylight flooded down upon them from the great glass walls and ceiling overhead. The marble basin of the fountain was easily the size of three large swimming pools, and the fountain itself was a kind of waterfall, cascading down a wall made to look like a cliff-face. To one side of the fountain there was a stretch of white sand arranged in the semblance of a beach, upon which a pirate camp had been pitched: a low red pavilion, a few barrels and kegs, and a treasure chest overflowing with chocolate coins in gold foil, marbles, colored quartz, licorice sticks, marshmallows, bananas, and rubber balls. At various places in the water, six small plaster statuettes of seventeenth-century tall ships rose from the water on sunken pedestals.

"This is a fine ship, Cap'n!" the bear called out to Gorilla.

"I thought you'd like it!"

They had been "at sea" for twenty minutes now. The tour of the castle after breakfast had not lasted very long. For one thing, Gorilla seemed to lose his way whenever he was busy talking and, since there was rarely a moment when he was not busy talking, he kept leading his two friends back to the same three rooms over and over. For another thing, it was really the fountain room he wanted to show them. Thus, when they had met Rolandus in one of the corridors, only a few moments after the dog had risen from his nap, Gorilla had delightedly cried out, "Ah, there's my trusty pilot!" The dog had shown little enthusiasm for a pirate's voyage just then, protesting that he would be needed to help prepare lunch, but Gorilla had insisted — or, at any rate, had said "please" roughly two dozen times very quickly and in his eagerest voice, until he was out of breath — and so, with only a stop in the nursery to collect some costumes and toy swords, the four of them had headed to the conservatory and down its spiral staircase to the end of the fountain where the boat was docked.

"Bring her alongside, Mr Roly!" Gorilla now called back as the boat approached one of the little plaster statuettes.

"You'll soon be walking the plank!" Porculina yelled with a wicked laugh. "Prepare to be boarded and relieved of your whole cargo!"

"Actually," said Gorilla, turning to the little pig, "robbing the ships isn't part of the game."

Porculina looked a little taken aback. "But isn't robbing ships what pirates do, Gor-Gor?" she asked in her normal voice.

"Well, bad pirates — *impolite* pirates — yes," said Gorilla. "But we're good pirates. We don't steal. We just ask for contributions, and we always say please, and then we say thank you kindly."

"Oh," said Porculina. Turning back towards the plaster ship, she called out, "Prepare to be boarded and asked for contributions!" Then she laughed wickedly again, just for effect.

"Remember to say 'Please,'" Gorilla whispered to her.

"Please," Porculina added, and laughed wickedly again, though not quite as convincingly as before.

As the ship drew alongside the statuette, Gorilla cried out, "Man the gun, Mr Pig!"

"Oh," said Porculina, "are we allowed to fire on the ship we're chasing? Wouldn't that be . . . impolite?"

"No," said Gorilla, "it's part of the game. And, anyway, we're not firing anything nasty at them. So" — he raised his voice again — "to that gun, Mister, and prepare to fire, or I'll have your stuffin' for pillows!"

"Aye-aye, Cap'n!" Porculina called out and ran to the little brass cannon to starboard, taking its pull-cord in her trotters.

"Mr Bear," Gorilla cried, "come for'ard and prepare to help me in boarding."

"Um, arr, right you be, Cap'n," Teddy answered, rising and going to Porculina's side.

"Steady now, Mr Pig," Gorilla said, "don't fire till I give the word. Steady . . . steady . . . hold your fire . . . steady . . . Now! Fire!"

"*Baaarrrooommm!*" yelled Porculina as she pulled the cord.

A medium-sized marshmallow flew from the mouth of the cannon in a graceful arc, bounced noiselessly off the statuette, and dropped into the water, where it began bobbing placidly.

"Hoorah!" shouted Porculina.

"Good shooting," remarked Teddy.

"A direct hit, Mr Pig!" bellowed Gorilla. "Mr Roly, bring us right up alongside!"

"Yes, sir," said the dog. "Or, rather, aye-aye, Cap'n."

The boat drifted up against the statuette and Gorilla, asking Teddy to hold him firmly by his sword belt, leaned over the side, reached around the back of the statuette, and brought back a small white sack with draw-strings that had evidently been hanging there from an unseen hook. "Thank you kindly," Gorilla called across to the statuette as Teddy pulled him back in. "All contributions are greatly appreciated." Then he turned to his shipmates. "Let's look at our booty," he said, and emptied the contents of the sack out on the deck. There were several chocolate coins in gold foil, two white linen napkins, five whistles, and seven rubber balls. "Look there, me hearties! Spanish doubloons, Jamaica cloth, and precious whistles and rubber balls from faraway . . . oh . . ." He picked up one of the balls and inspected it. "Taiwan! Well, let's get ashore and celebrate our famous victory! Grog for everyone!"

Rolandus saluted silently and steered them towards the pirate camp. When they came to the sandy bank, the three friends leaped out.

"With your permission, sir," called Rolandus from the helm as Gorilla skipped over to the pavilion, "or, rather, Cap'n, I'll take the launch — I mean, the ship — back to dock and go help in the kitchen. Or, if you prefer" — he looked upward, as if trying not to grimace — "get provisions. I hope, sir, miss," he added, looking from Teddy to Porculina, "you don't mind walking back along the outside of the fountain rather than sailing over."

"We quite understand," said Teddy.

"Don't you want any grog first, Mr Roly?" asked Gorilla, returning from the pavilion with four small green glass bottles of ginger ale in his arms.

"Very kind of you, sir," said the dog, "but we wouldn't want lunch to be late."

"Don't detain him," Porculina said with a faint urgency in her voice.

"Oh, all right, Mr Roly," said Gorilla. "Tell the story of our victory in the streets of Havana."

*   *   *

The three friends sat in the sand, talking loudly enough to be heard over the sound of the gushing fountain nearby, eating chocolate doubloons and bananas, and drinking ginger ale. Teddy had removed the eye patch and kerchief, but the other two were still in costume. Banana peels and gold foil wrappers lay scattered about in the sand.

"Maybe we should help Panda make up the rooms," Porculina suggested at one point. "If you're short of staff just now, she's all on her own."

"Capital idea, Piggles," replied Gorilla, "but it's no use. They never let me help them make the beds. It's always just 'Please, sir, if you keep bouncing on the mattresses, we'll never get finished,' or 'Oh, sir, you do look very terrifyingly like a ghost with the sheet over your head, but if we could just put it on the bed now,' or 'Pillowcases simply don't work as parachutes, sir,' and so on. And then Roly always comes and asks me to attend to something else. Anyway, it'll all be done by now. While we've been here, Panda will have cleared up all the rooms. She's very efficient."

"Gumdrops, I wish I were," Porculina said ruefully, putting another chocolate coin in her mouth. "I mean," she said, pausing for a swig of ginger ale, "I run a large cosmetics firm and everything, but all the book-keeping and organization and advertising is run by my staff. I'm just a 'big picture' sort of sow; I'm hopeless at all the little fiddly details. What are you thinking about, Teddykins?"

The little bear, who had indeed been lost in thoughts of his own, turned to his friends and smiled. "I'm thinking about our mystery," he said. "I'm just running it over in my mind and trying to decide who makes a plausible suspect and who doesn't. The problem is that interrogation tells us next to nothing, because everyone was supposedly in his or her room, or on his or her own, and there's no way of corroborating or contradicting any of it. And no one reports seeing or hearing anything that helps us. Only Ribbit and Jumping Bean were together and only they say they heard MacAw squorking next door, but if they were in on the heist that could just be a way of establishing an alibi. Not that I really suspect them. That little fellow's little more than a tadpole. And then . . . well, not to put too fine a point on it, just about everyone has a possible motive."

"Really?" asked Gorilla, delicately draping a banana peel over the end of his cutlass and trying unsuccessfully to twirl it around. "Why do you say that? I can't think of why anyone would want to take the treasure at all." He picked up the banana peel from the sand where it had fallen and placed it in the sack that he had brought back from the plaster statuette.

"I know," Teddy replied, "but you don't really care about things like money very much. You probably wouldn't even if you were poor rather than rich. You're just not a greedy sort of ape at all. But many people out there do think about money, quite a lot, and many have a real need for it."

"Am I rich?" asked Gorilla with a look of sincere curiosity on his face.

"Oh, yes, Gor-Gor," Porculina said, "I'd have to say you are. So am I. Teddy isn't, but he will be when his books sell. But many people don't have castles, you know, or pirate ships in the basements of their glass conservatories."

"I *have* noticed that," said Gorilla, nodding thoughtfully. "I've also noticed that many people don't have blue tricycles. I have one . . . though I'm not quite sure where it is just at the moment."

"If we run down the list of everyone here, apart from ourselves," said Teddy, "you can see that anyone might have had a reason for wanting to lift your treasure, and any of them might have had an opportunity. Of course, that's assuming the thieves aren't altogether different individuals, hiding out somewhere on the grounds. But in my experience that sort of thing is unlikely. It's hard to hide out undetected, even in a large place like this, for very long. But who knows?"

"Who indeed?" said Porculina.

"I think we have to assume that someone we know is involved," Teddy continued, "or that several someones are. The thing to do is go down the list in our heads, and try to sort out who's who."

"And then I leap in and draw wild conclusions," said Porculina with a small burst of enthusiasm, "or scratch my head and say, 'It's all beyond me, my dear old bear,' and things like that. Oh, this is delicious. Just caramel and cherries."

"Um, yes, I suppose so," said Teddy. "So let's start with the staff. I suppose Rolandus had the opportunity, and I can see why anyone in service might want to improve his . . ."

"Oh, that's silly," said Gorilla with a laugh. "Roly's looked after things here for years, like his father and grandfather before him. He's my strong right ear."

Porculina was dabbing her lips with one of the linen napkins that had come from the sack. "I don't think I've ever heard it put that way," she said.

"Oh, I don't really suspect Rolandus," said Teddy. "Even if he weren't so trustworthy, it would be unlikely. If he really wanted the treasure, he could get at it any time, without anyone noticing for a long time. Then, by the time the theft was discovered, there'd be no trace — maybe just a mysteriously unlocked window. It would be very odd for him to choose a night when a blizzard would make it impossible to get away cleanly with the prize. As for the rest of the staff here — well, for now it's just the pandas and Blue Bunny. The maid — Miss Panda, I should say — doesn't strike me as the sort, though one can't always tell. The chef is harder to read — a deep study, as so many toy pandas are — but if he was in the back at the time of the robbery, and the only way out that we know of would have taken him past his sister-in-law . . . Of course, if they were in it together . . ."

"Silly, silly, silly," said Gorilla, waving a hand dismissively. "Panda is as sweet as honey-butter on a currant muffin, and Pandus can't be a criminal. Anyone who's ever tasted his ginger-banana biscuits knows that. Only someone with a pure heart could possibly make anything so wonderful."

"Will there be any at lunch, do you think?" asked Porculina.

"Still, all I'm saying is that your chef has a motive," Teddy continued. "He wants his own restaurant. As for Blue Bunny . . ."

"Wonderful fellow," said Gorilla. "As rabbity a rabbit as you'd ever want to meet. Heart of pure tin."

"Gold," said Porculina.

"That too," said Gorilla. "Tin and gold and marzipan."

"He's a bit on the nervous side, though," Teddy remarked. "Does he have any special aspirations that you know of?"

"Oh," said Gorilla, "he breathes no more loudly than anyone else, as far as I can tell — though he does twitch his nose quite a bit."

"No, not *respirations*," said Teddy: "*aspirations*. You know, hopes and dreams and aims."

Gorilla thought for a moment. "He sometimes talks of having his own little cottage in the hills, surrounded by a large garden, full of carrots and celery and lettuces."

Teddy nodded slowly. "All right. That's something. Now, then, as for your guests, let's start with Woof. It's extremely unlikely he's involved, if you ask me. For one thing, I saw you invite him for dinner at the last moment, and I think this robbery had to be planned in advance in order for whoever it was to use the secret passage and to hide the treasure so quickly . . . Of course, as a handy man, he could have found the secret passage, and he and any accomplice he might have had here might have decided to take the opportunity . . . And, as politically he's an . . . whatever it is, he might have stolen your treasure just as a matter of political principle. But, on the other hand, he seems too sensible to choose a night with a blizzard, and he was there with Pigsy and me just as soon as the crash rang out, as you saw when you came along. What's more, he did nothing to delay us getting downstairs as quickly as possible. And, frankly, I trust him — he just seems trustworthy."

"Of course," said Gorilla, attempting to stand on his head in the sand, but rolling over on his back instead. "Woof's the sugar of the soil."

"Salt of the earth," Porculina said.

Gorilla brushed the sand from his ears and put his pirate's hat back on. "I don't know who'd want to eat salted earth," he said.

"And all the others have their possible motives too. The frogs said their extermination business was doing well, but the profits they cited weren't really very large. I can imagine how they might want to loosen the pinch."

"Who's pinched who, now?" asked Gorilla, tossing a blue rubber ball in the air and then failing to catch it, so that it bounced off his upturned nose.

"Who's pinched *whom*," Porculina corrected him.

"It's just an image," said Teddy. "I just mean they may be under financial pressure. And then there's Mr MacAw, who's openly admitted that he's been wanting to get your treasure into his museum for ages."

"That's right!" Porculina suddenly shouted in a strangely dramatic voice. "Why didn't I think of that, bear old chum? Clearly he's teamed up with a gang of French motorcar thieves to spirit the treasure away to his museum vaults in a large van disguised as a snowdrift. That's why they waited for the blizzard."

"What?" said Teddy with an utterly confused expression on his face.

"Just doing my bit as the slow-witted sidekick," said Porculina calmly. "Oh look, a marshmallow!"

"Right, sorry," said Teddy, raising a forefinger before him. "The problem is that, if Mr MacAw stole the treasure, he wouldn't be able to display it in his museum, because then everyone would know he was the thief. So stealing the treasure would actually thwart his plan — unless, of course, he only ever really wanted the treasure so that he could sell it. But that's unlikely, and — anyway — he's the only one of your guests who has any supporting witnesses to his alibi. The frogs heard him squorking."

"*Squorrrrggg!*" said Gorilla, in an attempt to imitate the sound as he imagined it.

"Then there's Cuttles," said Teddy. "Let me ask you, Gorilla, how well do his plays and poems actually do? In a financial sense, I mean."

"*Squooooorrrrkkkkkks!*" Gorilla continued.

"Gor-Gor," Porculina said, "please concentrate."

"Sorry," Gorilla said, putting the ball aside and looking at Teddy. "He tells me he's very famous and celebrated. He certainly seems like a very deep fellow to me."

"Yes," said Teddy, "but do people actually pay to watch his plays or buy his books? Because, from the little sample of them I've heard, they might be . . . well, ah, let's say, a little *too* deep for many people."

"That may be true," said Gorilla. "I can't get through any of them, they're so far over my head. And I did hear that his last play closed after only a third of a performance. Cuttles explained to me that it was too beautiful and tragical for the audience."

"Right," said Teddy, "as I suspected. So let's assume his writing hasn't made him rich. At the risk of repeating myself, everyone might have had a motive for . . ."

"But you've left someone out," interrupted Porculina. "What about Miss Raccoon?"

"Ah, well," said Teddy, clearing his throat several times and pointlessly adjusting his bowtie, "I suppose that's so. But I think we'd all agree that it's almost impossible to imagine anyone so famous and so . . . charming and delightful and . . . Well, I think we know it's unlikely she could have had anything to do with this business. Of course, just for the sake of argument, I suppose one could say that . . ." He paused and looked down at his feet.

"What?" asked Porculina after a moment.

"Well," Teddy said in a voice dripping with reluctance, "it's said that she's not getting all the roles in films she'd like to any more. And some writers on the cinema have said — well, it's ridiculous — have said that she's not really in demand the way she used to be . . . as if anyone would believe that. And there were some stories last month about recent difficulties she's been having in getting a film project of her own funded, a romantic musical comedy about Marie Antoinette with her in the lead. But that's all only so much talk."

"She really hasn't been in anything for a while, has she?" Porculina remarked casually. "I hear she's difficult to work with."

"Oh, nonsense," said Teddy. "You can see how perfectly enchanting she is. Stories like that just come from jealousy — people spreading rumors."

"Indeed," said Gorilla. "I like her. She's always very friendly, and she loves bananas, and she's pretty. She can't be a thief."

"That doesn't prove anything," said Porculina. "Teddy's a little smitten with her, and you like everybody, Gor-Gor. Anyway, it makes the point. They all have motives, and they all might have been involved. So, now, let me see." She put on her best thinking-hard expression for several seconds and then, in the same overly dramatic voice as before, said, "I have it, my dear old bear! Miss Raccoon, no doubt with the aid of an international criminal band of magicians and acrobats, many of them stoats or weasels, had the treasure flown away in large air-balloons, launched from the battlements of the castle. It's the only possible explanation."

This time, Teddy was prepared and played along. "No, my good and faithful pig, there are a few obvious flaws in that theory, which I will enumerate for you as we walk back and try to find Rolandus. Right now, we need to get some flashlights — torches, that is — and go have another look at that secret passage from the treasure room. A theory's occurred to me — it came to me when you mentioned magicians, actually — and I want to test it out before lunch. Oh, and I am not smitten with Miss Raccoon, whatever you think. I'm just an admirer of her work. Let's go."

So the three friends gathered up their things, placed their litter in the sack, and set off around the outside of the great fountain in the direction of the spiral stairway.

CHAPTER 9

A Rising Tide

THEY FOUND ROLANDUS IN THE KITCHEN AND HE procured each of them a flashlight from a storeroom nearby. Then the three friends returned to the treasure room, where everything was exactly as it had been immediately after the robbery. Teddy had asked Rolandus not to let anyone disturb the scene of the crime. Even the heavy secret door beside the fireplace still stood open into the inky darkness of the passage beyond, although Rolandus had closed the door at the other end once the contentedly snoring Laird of Castle MacGorilla had been carried in from the maze the night before.

"Look," said Gorilla, shaking his head, "it's still there."

"What?" asked Porculina.

"That large unseemly dark and empty not-thereness in the wall," said Gorilla. "It just doesn't go with the rest of the room at all."

"We can always shut the door when we're finished investigating," said Teddy, "but right now we have to inspect every inch of that corridor."

"What are we looking for, then?" asked Porculina, approaching the mouth of the passage and peering in.

Teddy came to her side. "Well, when we went outside last night, we saw footprints in the snow leading out, but none leading in. So the robbers must have gotten into the treasure room from inside the castle. Now, maybe they sneaked in through the sitting room, but that would be pretty daring and unlikely. On top of that, there was no way of getting the treasure out through the sitting room without being detected, especially with all those large oil paintings — think of the time it would take and the noise it would make — but also there was no way to take the treasure out the other end of the passage without leaving far more evidence in the snow, and without at least two thieves doing the work. But there was only one pair of tracks, heading off to the maze. And then, of course, the door was locked from the inside and the window hadn't been opened in ages, apparently, and the snow beneath the sill was undisturbed."

"So what does all of that tell us?" asked the little pig.

"That there's only one way the treasure could have disappeared so completely. I think there's another secret door in there somewhere, leading somewhere else. I think the thieves may have used that door to get into the secret passage here from somewhere inside the castle, and I think they definitely used it to get the treasure out of here and into some hiding place on the estate, until it's safe to move it again. And, you remember, Rolandus said that all that racket last night almost sounded to him like heavy objects falling down a flight of stairs. Well, I think that may be just what it was, at least in part. I think our thieves were hurrying to get the treasure out of here and down a secret stairway, and one or both of them slipped and sent it all crashing down."

Porculina turned her eyes from Teddy and gazed excitedly into the corridor. "Custard and crumpets! Why didn't I think of that . . . er, my dear old bear? But what about the display stand lying on its side? I thought that was what made the noise."

"It was quite a noise," said Teddy, "with more than one source. Perhaps one of the thieves knocked over the pedestal, which caused the other to drop an armful of treasure in surprise, or perhaps the other way around, or . . ."

"What perfectly clumsy robbers," said Porculina with a smirk.

"Oh, now, I drop things and trip over pedestals and things all the time," Gorilla remarked cheerfully, turning on his flashlight and beginning to make figures-eight on the ceiling with its beam. "You mustn't mock them." He made a few soft "*vroom-vroom*" noises to himself.

"Really, Gor-Gor," said Porculina, "they're robbers. And one of them viciously attacked your dear little round head when your back was turned and you were utterly, utterly defenseless. You needn't be so nice about them. I tell you," she added, her voice rising in pitch and volume, "when those barbarians are finally caught, mockery will be the least of their worries. They'll soon learn just how *very bitter are the wages of crime!*" These last words came out in a surprisingly shrill squeal. Porculina immediately looked abashed, cleared her throat, and said, in a softer voice, "Sorry about that. I was trying to give it a little dramatic *oomph*."

"Now, now," said Gorilla, raising an admonishing finger as he politely slipped between his friends, "you were always the one at school who used to say we must try to think the best of everyone. And we should always practice what we screech." Then he walked forward, into and down the corridor, wiggling his flashlight up and down as he did so. "Tally-ho, you two!" he called back over his shoulder. "It's all snouts on deck!"

Porculina and Teddy watched him for a moment.

"He's certainly good at turning a phrase," the little pig said in an admiring tone.

"Yes," said the little bear with a nod, "and at turning it inside out."

Gorilla, jauntily striding down the passage and gaily whistling, was already out of sight; only the dancing beam of his flashlight was visible. Teddy and Porculina exchanged glances, shrugged, turned on their flashlights, and followed.

* * *

The three friends now had time to look over the corridor carefully, as they had been unable to do the night before. It had an eerie feel to it on account of the darkness, but was really a very simple affair, about forty feet in length and ten feet across, with a ceiling about seven feet high. The mortar in the brickwork appeared to be seamless. Certainly, they could find no sign of another hidden door, no matter how closely they looked.

"Well," said Teddy, "if there's a door, there must be a handle, and the only handles visible here are these torch brackets. So let's give them a try." In all there were ten brackets, midway up the walls, five on either side of the passage, and Teddy reached for the one nearest him. He tried to pull it out and, when that failed, to turn it now one way, now the other. "Nothing here," he said.

They went together from one bracket to another, testing each in turn. In a few minutes, they had eliminated all of those on one side of the corridor and two on the other, but when they came to the third — situated midway along the wall — Teddy was able to pull it out about two inches; it was affixed by only a slender iron rod that slid out surprisingly smoothly from the bricks. All at once, there was a sound of springs and of grinding granite, of the sort they had heard the previous night when they had opened the secret door at the far end of the tunnel, and a three foot wide section of the wall, just to the left of the bracket, began to swing open and away from them.

"Pepper jelly!" Porculina exclaimed. "That's remarkable."

"Now that *is* a surprise," said Gorilla. "I never knew my castle had so many of those things about."

114

"Here are our stairs," said Teddy, shining his light onto a long flight of granite steps leading downward from the door. It was about three feet wide and was enclosed by walls and a low ceiling.

"You know," said Porculina, "it's not totally dark down there." And, in fact, there was a soft gauzy glow below them, about forty feet down, apparently spilling in from somewhere beyond the bottom stairs. "Shouldn't it be pitch black?"

"I suppose not," said Teddy. "Gorilla, please don't shout out to see if someone's down there."

With a slightly embarrassed look, Gorilla let the hand that he had just cupped around his mouth fall back to his side. "Why? Is it bad etiquette?" he asked in a worried tone.

"As a rule, yes," said Teddy, "at least when you're tracking criminals. Let's just go down and look around, trying not to make any noise. I doubt anyone's there right now, but if someone is, we don't want to warn him we're coming."

"But what if he's serving tea," asked Gorilla, "and we just show up unannounced? That'll put him in a pretty sticky social situation. You should always let people know you're coming for a visit before you just drop in."

"Oh, Gor-Gor," said Porculina with a sigh, "you just don't read enough mysteries. This isn't a visit; it's a chase. We're on the trail of malefactors — you know, dastardly villains and pitiless poltroons. We have to sneak up on them. We just have to. It's . . . it's what they'd expect."

Gorilla thought about this for a moment and then said, in a cautious tone, "Well, if it's what they'd expect. But I do so hate being impolite."

"No fear of that," said Teddy. "You're the soul of civility. But she's right. I'll take the lead, and we all need to walk quietly."

The three friends descended the stairs, not speaking but with flashlights shining. The air was chilly and felt slightly damp, and their delicate, cottony footfalls echoed ever so slightly in stony whispers all around them. When they reached the bottom, they found themselves at the entrance of a large room, into which the pearly light of winter poured down in a great fan from about thirty feet above. It was dim in here, but sufficiently bright for them to extinguish their flashlights.

"It's carpeted!" said Porculina in surprise, as her eyes adjusted to her surroundings.

And, indeed, a large square red carpet, adorned with blue and golden and green figures of birds and vines and trees, covered much of the floor of the huge circular chamber in which they found themselves. In all, the space was perhaps sixty feet across. There were eight large leathern armchairs, clearly very old, randomly distributed around the room, as well as four reading tables and — standing across the room from where they had entered — a large, handsome desk with a flat top covered in green leather; and on the desk and on each of the tables there was a single kerosene lantern made of amber-colored crystal. Around the walls, at regular intervals, were five other entryways, leading off in various directions, and in the spaces between them were several old and large bookcases, filled with countless leather-bound tomes.

"Oh, so *here* it is," said Gorilla casually. "I knew it was around somewhere."

Teddy and Porculina turned and stared at him.

"Here *what* is?" asked Porculina.

"My great uncle Robert's hidden library, of course," Gorilla answered. "I knew it might turn up some place or other. I just didn't know he had left it lying around here. Oh look," he said, pointing upward, "I know what that is."

Teddy and Porculina turned their eyes to the ceiling. It was much smaller in diameter than the floor of the room — maybe no more than ten feet — because the walls sloped evenly inward from the ground upward, narrowing the space continuously as they rose. At the center of the ceiling was a circular skylight, beyond whose milkily frosted glass they could easily make out a hazy silhouette of grating in a cobweb pattern.

"That skylight, do you mean?" said Teddy.

"Yes," said Gorilla. "That's one of the grates on the little dam-like thing in the middle of my little lake on the south side of the castle. Just a sort of brick thing sticking out of the water, called a sluice-gate or something like that, with water flowing into it through bars on one side. I've boated over there often — or Roly's boated me over. There are five grates on top of it, just like that one. I think that dam's where the water flows down from the lake into the underground stream. Apparently — Woof explained this to me once — that's where the water in the hothouse fountain comes from, through a . . . I can't recall exactly . . . a flitteration system, I think."

They all lowered their eyes again.

"You both understand, now," Gorilla continued, looking at them and speaking to them as though they were small children, "up there the grating is underfoot if you're standing on the dam, but here it's overhead. That's very confusing, I know — at least, it confuses me — but I think that's because we're underground. If you think about it, it makes sense. At least, I think it does. We're down here, you see . . ."

"Yes, yes, I think we understand," said Teddy. "It makes perfect sense. We're under the lake. And I suppose the water flows under the other grates, and on all sides of that one up there, into the filter system for your fountain room, so no one would ever guess that the central gate is actually a window into a hidden library. Very clever."

"But you knew about this place?" Porculina asked Gorilla.

"Well," said Gorilla, walking over to one of the armchairs and settling into it, "my great uncle Robert was a funny old ape, and years ago he decided to take all the rare and precious manuscripts in the castle library — you know, records of the castle's doings, maps, the diaries of the famous MacGorillas of yore, his favorite cook books — and put them somewhere safe. Somewhere, he said, where the 'Sassenach beasties'll never find them.' He was always sure the Sassenachs would come one day to steal the castle's cook books and so forth. 'Sassenach' means 'English,' by the way. I think it's French."

"No," said Porculina, "it's Gaelic."

117

"But 'Gaelic' is Scottish for 'French,' I think," Gorilla replied.

"Ah, no . . ." Teddy began, but then changed his mind and said, "Anyway, he built this secret library?"

"He said he did," said Gorilla. "Mind you, most of the clan just assumed he'd lost the books and was too embarrassed to tell us. But I believed him. I knew it would turn up one day. I mean, I've lived in the castle all my life, and I'm always finding things I haven't seen before . . . or don't recall seeing . . . balls, books, secret hallways. I mean, just think about that large not-thereness upstairs in the treasure room — I'd never noticed that before at all."

"But that's because it wasn't there until . . ." Porculina began, but then thought better of it. "So," she said, sweeping her arms around her, "all these books have been hidden here since then. But he couldn't have built all this without anyone noticing. And it looks ancient."

"Well," said Gorilla, "there are plenty of stories about underground caverns and chambers and things going back to the Great Gorilla himself, so maybe Uncle Robbie just converted this one into a library. He knew all the old maps of the castle and they would have told him if there was a secret room lying about. It's rather nice, isn't it? Do you see any toys around?"

"Where do you suppose all these other passages lead to?" asked Porculina.

"Somewhere else, I imagine," said Gorilla, beginning to bounce up and down gently in his seat. "I say, this is a jolly chair."

"We'd better check," said Teddy. "If they lead to other parts of the castle, then they may lead us to our criminals."

"This would be a wonderful place for a bagpipes recital," Gorilla remarked, "or a birthday party. Or — oh, I know, hide-and-seek." Gorilla's voice had become suddenly eager and he moved forward to the edge of his chair. "Did you two know that hide-and-seek is the competitive sport at which my family most excels?"

"No," said Porculina, her curiosity all at once piqued, "I had no idea."

"Hide-and-seek is a competitive sport?" asked Teddy.

"It is here in Scotland, yes," said Gorilla. "It's part of what we call the Highland Games. Many MacGorillas have taken top prizes. One of my illustrated relatives, Ian MacGorilla, once won the highest marks in the contest ever. I was just a little tot of an ape in those days, but I remember it well. The games were being hosted here at the castle that year, and several other contestants were able to remain undetected for as much as an hour or more. But once the appointed seeker — the previous year's champion — had closed his eyes and counted to twenty, he couldn't find my great-great uncle Ian at all. After three hours, he was joined by three lieutenant seekers, but still they couldn't find my great-great uncle. And, even when everybody had joined in, even the competition judges, they were still unable to find him *for three weeks*."

"Peanuts and popcorn!" cried Porculina in a tone of rapt amazement. "Weeks? That's amazing. Where was he hiding?"

"Well, actually," said Gorilla with a proud smile, "he wasn't hiding at all — not as such. You see, a little while after going to hide, he had forgotten about the contest altogether and had left for his annual vacation in France. But when he got back the judges gave him the prize, along with a certificate of special distinction. He had eluded them longer than anyone else ever, they said. Oh, it was a great day for the clan, I can tell you. They even erected a statue of him in the maze. It shows him eating a sandwich at a French café, and the inscription reads 'Ian the Elusive, Champion of All Scotland.' It really is rather magnificent."

"You have such an heroic — such a *glamorous* — family history," said Porculina with a sigh of admiration.

"Yes," said Teddy, "it's . . . very vivid. But we really must get back to the task at hand." He walked over to one of the mysterious entryways, and peered into it. After a few seconds, he turned his flashlight on and shined its beam ahead of him. "It's another flight of stairs," he said, "leading upward."

He went to each of the other entryways in turn. Each led to a stairway, three leading upward, but one leading downward, and all of them into impenetrable darkness.

"Well, then," said Teddy, returning to his friends, "we'd probably better investigate each of them in turn."

*   *   *

The first four flights of stairs were similar to the one by which Teddy, Porculina, and Gorilla had descended to the secret library, though three of them were much longer and had a few twists and turns along the way. Teddy led the way each time, with Porculina close behind him breathlessly uttering things like "Lemons and lollipops!" or "Treacle and tarts!" and Gorilla bringing up the rear, sometimes making train noises and on one occasion quietly calling out, "Slow ahead, elephants on the tracks!" Each stairway, however, led to a dead end: a door of bricks, like the one they had found in the secret corridor above, on large iron hinges, but locked fast and with no visible latch or handle on this side.

"Well," Teddy remarked when they had returned from their fourth expedition, "I don't know the castle well enough even to guess where those other doors might lead, and I doubt I'd be able to even if I were familiar with every room in the place. There must be some way of opening them from here, but it's well hidden. Otherwise, one would risk getting locked in." He looked about the library walls for several moments thoughtfully. "I don't know, but I think the second flight leads up to about the level of the downstairs portions of the castle, the first and the third up to the main level, and the fourth up to a higher floor, maybe where our bedrooms are. But I can't tell for certain, and it's going to take some time to work that out. I think we'll need Rolandus and Woof to help us."

"Shall we investigate the last stairway, then?" asked Porculina.

Teddy turned his eyes to it. "Yes, of course. Going down into darkness feels somewhat more dangerous to me, I have to say . . ." He paused.

"Well, we're all together," said Gorilla cheerfully. "Nothing to fear. Three for all and all for the good!" He strode across the room to the last entryway, looked back at his friends with an encouraging smile, turned

120

again to the stairs, stepped down, and promptly fell forward and rolled head-over-heels out of sight. A series of soft thumps and exclamations of "Oof!" and "Ouch!" and "I say!" rose up from the darkness for a few seconds, diminishing rapidly in volume, and then there was silence.

"Gor-Gor!" cried Porculina, dashing over to the stairway on her short legs, with Teddy close behind. "You poor unlucky monkey!" she called down into the darkness. "Are you all right?"

There were a few tense moments of silence, but then Gorilla's jovial voice floated up from below: "Do be careful, you two. It's easy to take a tumble on those stairs. I nearly did myself."

Teddy and Porculina both took deep breaths of relief and, switching on their flashlights, went down the stairs. In all, the descent was about twenty feet, at the bottom of which they found themselves in another circular chamber, but this one maybe only fifteen feet in diameter and twelve feet high, without a skylight, and entirely empty apart from Gorilla, who was sitting in the middle of the bare stone floor by a large grated drain with his head resting pensively on one fist and his flashlight resting by his side, its beam shining away from them. Directly across from the stairs they had just descended was another entryway, beyond which their lights clearly showed yet another flight of steps, this time leading upward again.

"I have to say," Gorilla remarked after a moment, "that this is the most boring room I've found in the castle so far."

"It's certainly not very cheery," Porculina said.

"I suppose," said Teddy, "that we should keep moving on. Those stairs over there must lead somewhere too."

"What are those?" asked Porculina. She was shining her light upward, and moving it around the edges of the flat brick ceiling. At regular intervals, high up on the walls, there were four rectangular openings in the brickwork, each no more than a foot high and half a foot wide.

"I don't know," answered Teddy. "Perhaps vents for keeping the air fresh down here."

"Gorillas aren't actually monkeys, by the way," Gorilla remarked. "I say, do you think those other stairs might lead to something nicer than this?"

"We can only look," said Teddy.

They made their way up the staircase, which was not quite as long as the one they had just come down. And indeed, as Gorilla had hoped, these stairs most certainly did lead to something nicer.

"Raspberry marmalade!" Porculina gasped as she reached the top step, just a few steps behind Teddy, and saw what he was looking at in the beam of his flashlight.

It was a room only slightly larger than the one they had just left, but it was anything but empty. At its center, heaped haphazardly in a great gleaming and glistening mound, as if flung there hastily and care-lessly, was the great treasure of Castle MacGorilla: gold and silver, coins and chains and brooches, glittering gems pouring from caskets lying open on their sides, the two magnificent swords in their gorgeous scabbards, jeweled scepters and the great crown encrusted with diamonds, rubies, and emeralds, and — leaning up against the walls on all sides — all the precious framed portraits. In the darkness of the room, lit only by the three flashlights, the hoard shone out with an almost ghostly glow.

The three friends stood in silence for some moments.

Then, at last, Gorilla spoke: "Well, *here* it is. Fancy that. What a fuss we've been making over nothing. The treasure wasn't stolen. Someone just put it here, probably by mistake. Well, so, that's taken care of — and just in time for lunch."

Teddy closed his eyes for a moment, shook his head, and then said, very gently, "Ah, no, not precisely. You see, the treasure *was* stolen, that's for certain. This is just where the thieves hid it until they could get it away without detection."

"Oh," said Gorilla, looking a little uncertain. "Are you quite sure? Let's not leap to wild conclusions, now. I mean, I'm misplacing things all the time."

"Yes, but if you think about it," Teddy said, "I mean, really think about the sequence of events last night, what with the chase in the maze, and the disorder in the treasure room — well, you see, it clearly is a case of theft."

"Oh, well," said Gorilla, a little reluctantly, "I suppose you'd know about these things." He looked at the treasure for several seconds more, clucking his tongue thoughtfully in his mouth. "Still," he finally added, "I'm sure they won't do it again. After all, it's not a very interesting — oh, look, what's that?" He walked over to the wall about five feet to his left. "Look at this. I wonder what it does."

In the beam of Gorilla's flashlight, Teddy and Porculina now saw what had caught their friend's attention. Protruding at an upward angle from a dark slotted plate in the bricks was a small lever, fashioned from some dark metal and capped with an old and very worn wooden handle. Just above it was a brass plaque that appeared to bear an inscription, but that only Gorilla was near enough to read.

"What does it say?" asked Teddy. Then: "No, for goodness' sake, don't pull . . . !"

But, before he could finish, Gorilla had taken hold of the lever and yanked it downward. All at once, a portentous sound of heavy shifting metal plates came through the walls, as if somewhere in the depths of the granite some immense door had been opened, and immediately there was a great spluttering and gurgling and splashing noise rising up from somewhere below, which quickly became a loud, continuous, rushing roar, echoing all around them.

"Oh, dear!" cried Porculina, running to Gorilla's side. "Oh, crumbly crumbles! What have you done, Gor-Gor?"

Teddy ran after her, yelling, "Quick, pull the lever up again!"

"Hmm," said Gorilla, "that's very interesting." He was reading the plaque now. "Let's see, it says here, 'Open the Sluices and Fill the Cistern.' I wonder what that means."

"Please," Teddy cried, "push it back!"

"Oh, very well," said Gorilla casually. He took hold of the lever and lifted it upward in its slot again. The sound of water continued unabated.

The little bear took hold of the lever himself and shifted it downward and upward several times. Nothing happened.

"What cistern is it talking about, Teddy?" Porculina asked in a frantic voice.

Teddy looked about him wildly for a moment, then paused and listened, and then turned to the stairs. "That room down there," he said, pointing urgently to the doorway. "That must be what those vents up by the ceiling were. Come on, quickly, maybe we can get out before it fills." He dashed to the stairs and began to descend them, but paused after only two steps.

Porculina, who had followed close after him, now almost collided with him. "Why have you stopped?"

"It's too late," Teddy replied somberly.

Porculina looked over his shoulder. The enclosed stairwell was now full of a soft undulating and flickering golden light, because the beam of Teddy's flashlight was being reflected upward in all directions from the surface of the water that had already filled the lower third of the stairs, and that was still visibly and rapidly rising.

"My, my," said Gorilla, who had now joined his friends and was gazing over Teddy's other shoulder, "that's very inconvenient."

Teddy stepped up into the room again and placed his paw upon his brow. He looked distinctly worried.

Gorilla, however, continued to gaze down the stairway. "I wonder," he said, tapping his lower lip with his thumb. "Yes, I do wonder. If you two will just pardon me for a moment," he said and began to descend the steps.

"Where are you going?" Porculina cried. "Gor-Gor, come back! Oh, pickles!"

"I'll be careful," Gorilla called back to her without turning around. "I just need to check something. It may be very important."

Teddy and Porculina both went to the top of the stairs and aimed their lights down at the figure of Gorilla, who was cautiously making his way to the rising surface of the water.

"Old fellow," Teddy called down, "you can't get out through all of that."

"Now, now," Gorilla yelled back, still without turning, "I'll be with you in a moment." Then, when he reached the last dry step, he delicately extended one of his stout short legs before him and dipped his toes in the water. Then he quickly withdrew his foot and, shaking his head gravely, turned around and began to ascend the stairs again. When he had rejoined his friends, he looked at them both with an ominous expression. "It's just as I feared," he said: "It's the wet kind of water."

For a moment, Teddy and Porculina stared at Gorilla blankly, as if dazed.

"That's what you went to check, is it?" said Teddy finally.

"Yes," said Gorilla solemnly. "Somebody had to. Oh, well. I suppose you both know what this means."

Porculina screamed, so suddenly and so loudly that the other two jumped. Teddy momentarily lost his grip on his flashlight, but caught it before it hit the floor.

"Yes, I know what it means!" she cried out in a voice full of the bleakest anguish. Her eyes were wide, her lips were trembling, her flashlight shook violently in her trotter. "I know exactly what it means! We're going to miss lunch!"

CHAPTER 10

The Trap Is Set

"NO, I DON'T THINK IT'S AS BAD AS ALL THAT," said Gorilla to Porculina. "We may be a bit late for lunch, but that's nothing to worry about."

"Nothing?" gasped the little pig in a desperate voice. "How can you say that? Don't you know that it's a physiological fact that, unless soft toys get six or seven square meals and several snacks each day, at regular intervals, they shrink down to the size and consistency of dishrags?"

"No, no," said Teddy distractedly, "that's a myth. Please, whatever happens, we absolutely mustn't panic. Let's think."

"What I meant," Gorilla continued, "is that we may get very wet. And I don't mean wet in a warm and sudsy way, as when you take a bath, but in a cold and somewhat muddy way, as when you fall into the lake because you're trying to play leapfrog in your boat, but without warning Roly before trying to vault over him, or because you drop your ball over the side and you see it floating just out of reach and you stretch out to get it and . . ."

"Yes, yes," said Porculina, still trembling, "I understand."

"Well, when that happens," Gorilla said, "it gets right down into your stuffing and seams, and then you can't just take a bath, you need to be . . . well . . . you need to be . . . *laundered.*"

"Oh, crumbs!" cried Porculina.

"Gorilla, you're making it worse," Teddy said. "Look, we need to think . . . to look around . . ."

"I'm just saying," said Gorilla, "so that we're all prepared. There's no other way. Otherwise . . . well, I don't like to bring up the matter of mildew, but . . ."

"Gorilla, I'm going to cry if you don't stop," Porculina moaned. "Anyway, that's not the problem. I can bear being laundered, but I've never missed a meal in my life."

"And then it's out on the clothesline, hanging from your ears till you're dry. Actually, that part can be rather fun. One has loads of time to think about things. Of course, Roly will have to string the line in the hothouse, I suppose, since we'd freeze outside just now . . ."

Teddy was now standing at the top of the stairs again. "You know, I don't think the water will get into this room," he said after a moment. "I think it must shut off before that. I didn't see any sign of water damage in the library, and we're almost as high up at this end. So I think the level is supposed to flood the cistern and the stairs at either end, so as to cut this room off, but not to rise any higher."

The sound of the rushing water continued, however, as vigorously as before, and the water in the stairwell was now only three steps from the top.

Porculina, coming to Teddy's side, said, "Are you sure?"

"Um, yes," said the little bear, "at least, I think so." Then, after a moment's hesitation, he added, more firmly, "Yes, definitely."

"Oh, well," Gorilla said, shining his flashlight around the walls, "that's all right then."

"But we'll be cut off!" Porculina said anxiously. "We can't stay here. There's nothing to . . . nothing to eat!"

"Oh, something will turn up," Gorilla said cheerfully. "Something always does."

Teddy walked back into the room and stared at the treasure. "She's right, you know," he said. "We really can't swim down there and then across that lower chamber and up the other staircase. I mean, you'd have to be a powerful swimmer for that, and we're . . . well, we're soft toys. And it's just not in our . . ."

Suddenly, a low rumbling metallic clash reverberated through the walls of the room, and all at once the sound of rushing water ceased.

"There," said Teddy, "just as I predicted."

"Oh, but Teddy," Porculina said, still gazing into the stairwell, "the water's right up to the top step. Oh, we're never going to eat again."

"Now, now, then," said Gorilla, with robust heartiness, "let's not be silly about this. It's simply time to start looking around."

"For what?" asked Porculina in a hopeless tone.

Gorilla shook his head fondly and gave her his most patient smile. "Well, isn't that obvious, Piggles?"

Porculina shook her head.

"Why, you silly old thing, for a submarine, of course."

The little pig took three steps away from the stairs and towards him. "But, Gor-Gor, why would there be a submarine down here?"

Gorilla's expression became even kindlier. "Silly, silly old Piggles," he said gently, "you're not thinking. The proper question is why *wouldn't* there be a submarine down here? You see, it's so much nicer if you put it that way."

For a moment, all was silence, except for the gentle slapping of the water against the ledge of the top step. Porculina's look of dismay had been replaced by one of sheer bafflement. But then she turned to Teddy and nodded slowly. "You know, he's right," she said. "It's much nicer that way. Listen: Why wouldn't there be a submarine? See?"

Teddy looked about him. "Well, for one thing, because this isn't a very big room here, and we'd probably see a submarine if there were one anywhere about."

Gorilla merely shook his head with an expression of gentle exasperation. "Now, now . . ." he began.

"But, you know," Teddy continued, "Gorilla is right when he says we should start looking around. I mean, if there's a way of opening the sluices on this side of the cistern, shouldn't there be a way of draining the cistern on this side too? There was a drain on the floor down there, if you recall. I mean, surely the whole point of having a cistern there is so that it can be filled to prevent anyone from finding this room or getting to it, and if someone were hiding over here . . ."

Gorilla clapped his hands. "I'll bet this is the secret treasure room," he said.

"If someone . . . if . . ." Teddy paused and looked at Gorilla. "There's a secret treasure room? One you knew about?"

"Oh, just stories, like Uncle Robbie's library. It all goes back to the days of Bonnie Prince Someone-or-Other — a very important fellow, I believe — and it's said there's a secret room in the castle that was built for hiding the treasure if necessary, or hiding Bonnie Prince Someone-or-Other, who was on the run from the English or the French or someone, and there was a way of flooding the antechamber so no one could find it. All the MacGorillas know the story."

"Ah," said Teddy. "Well, perhaps that explains . . ."

"Do you happen to know what Pandus made for lunch today?" Porculina suddenly interjected.

Teddy held up his paw. "Wait, I think we may be able to find that out for ourselves. At any rate, let's try. Let's look about the room to see if we can find anything at all that might release the water. A switch, a lever, a chain — anything at all."

"Oh, that sounds jolly," said Gorilla.

So the three friends scattered to different parts of the room and began carefully inspecting every inch of wall, occasionally tipping the oil portraits away from the bricks and shining their flashlights behind them. At first, no one spoke, but after five minutes Teddy called out, "Anything? Either of you?"

"Nothing here," Porculina answered.

"No, not to speak of," Gorilla said.

They continued to search for a few minutes more, and then Teddy, still having found nothing, walked back into the center of the room, stopping near the treasure. "Nothing yet?"

Porculina stood up straight from where she had been crouching down to peer behind a painting and joined Teddy. "Nothing," she said in a despairing voice.

Gorilla turned to his friends. "I can't say I've found anything interesting either." He walked to the center of the room as well. "Just bricks and a rather nice cobweb. Oh, and that other lever there."

Teddy and Porculina both suddenly stiffened. "What lever?" they cried, almost simultaneously.

"Oh, just that one there on the wall," said Gorilla, nonchalantly waving his hand over his shoulder. "It's just like the other one, except that its plaque says, 'Seal Sluices and Drain Cistern.' It's rather dull."

"Oh, dear!" Porculina cried just as Teddy was crying, "My goodness!" and both rushed past Gorilla.

"That's it!" Teddy cried. "Where is it?"

"Oh, behind that portrait of Duncan MacGorilla. He's the one with the bagpipes and the top hat with a lollipop sticking out of its band. Are you sure that's the lever you want, though?"

"Goodness, Gor-Gor," said Porculina, momentarily glancing back at him as Teddy began to tilt the portrait away from the wall, "sometimes I wonder if you're all there."

Gorilla considered this for a moment. Then he began gently patting

131

himself around the head and sides and legs, finally pinching each of his toes. "No, I seem to be all here," he said.

"Here it is!" Teddy called out triumphantly. "And here it goes!" He pulled down on the lever.

Once again, they heard the sound of a large metal plate sliding back, but this time it seemed to rise up to them from much farther down than before, and then there was the unmistakable noise of great quantities of water flowing rapidly somewhere far below the floor on which they stood.

Porculina ran to the stairs, and after a few moments cried out in delight, "It's going down! The water level is going down! And quickly! Oh, wonderful, we're . . . we're not going to miss lunch after all!"

*   *   *

In all it took fewer than ten minutes for the cistern to drain. When the three friends had heard the last of the water disappearing, with a sound reminiscent of a bathtub emptying, they made their way down the stairs — which were now very wet and slick underfoot — across the floor of the lower chamber, up the opposite flight of stairs, across the hidden library, and up the stairs to the hidden corridor again. There, Teddy pushed the torch bracket back into the wall, and the door swung shut.

"Well," said Porculina once they were back in the treasure room, "I suppose we should get a party together to bring the treasure up after lunch."

"Oh, no," said Teddy, "we mustn't tell anyone what we've found — not the secret door, or the library, or certainly the treasure. No one, that is, except for Rolandus — I'll tell him privately when I can get a chance. And Woof too."

"But why keep it a secret?" asked Porculina.

"It's not nice to keep secrets," said Gorilla.

"Yes, but our mystery's not solved yet," Teddy said, turning off his flashlight and staring thoughtfully at his feet. "And, frankly, we don't have much time. What we may have now, though, is a way of catching our thieves. Anyway, I think it's just about time for lunch. So, please . . ."

132

But he stopped, because he had lifted his eyes and seen that only Gorilla was there beside him. The door into the sitting room was standing open, and from somewhere beyond the sitting room came the rapidly receding sound of small galloping trotters.

*   *   *

"You know," said Porculina, after swallowing the last bite of her dessert (a banana tart), "this isn't quite how I pictured our mystery going at all, really. I mean, not to complain, but bitter broth and stale bread! The robbery and the chase in the darkness was all very exciting, all right, and you don't get trapped by rising waters in the depths of the earth every day, but let's be honest — things are moving along just a little too smartly. The treasure was taken last night, and we've found it before lunch. At this rate, we'll have it wrapped up by teatime. There's just no . . . well, no suspense."

Teddy shrugged and looked about him. He, Porculina, and Gorilla were seated at the same table at which they had breakfasted, and all the other guests had also resumed their stations of the morning, almost as if their seats had been permanently assigned. With all the electricity still out, this was the room with the most light, so lunch had been served here rather than in the customary dining room on the west side; and, given the shortage of staff, the meal had again been laid out as a buffet. Only Rolandus was in attendance, making sure that everything was up to his standards.

"Well?" Porculina continued. "A shrug isn't a reply, you know. How are we going to make things more interesting? The lunch was luscious, though, wasn't it?"

"I think there's plenty of suspense," Teddy said after a moment — "more than I care for, really. We still haven't the faintest idea who stole the treasure in the first place. Finding it wasn't hard, because the theft was a foolish venture to begin with. The thieves chose the worst possible time for their escapades, so it stood to reason that they'd hidden the treasure somewhere nearby. That's what I was trying to explain to you when you tore off for lunch. What I think we should do is gather the guests together, along with the staff if possible, in about half an hour, and tell them that we've discovered a doorway leading down from the secret corridor, and that we intend to go explore it later today. Then . . ."

"No, no, that will never do," said Gorilla shaking his head and wagging a finger.

"Why ever not?" asked Porculina.

"Because we've explored it already, and we don't want to tell a lie. Liars never whisper, you know."

"Uh, yes," said Teddy, "I think that's 'liars never prosper.' But you do have a point. Dishonesty is always unworthy of soft toys of good character. But I wasn't going to tell them that we *hadn't* already gone down the stairs; I simply wasn't going to mention that we had."

"Why tell them anything at all, though?" asked Porculina. "What's the point?"

"The point is," said Teddy, leaning a little closer, and dropping his voice to little more than a murmur, "that we'll then go directly down to the library, along with Rolandus, and hide ourselves — you can do this, Gorilla, honestly, if you just don't start whistling, or bouncing a rubber ball in the air, or laughing at jokes you tell yourself — and wait."

"For whom?" asked Porculina.

"The thieves," said Teddy.

"But why would the thieves go to the library?" asked Gorilla. "Do you think they might want something to read?"

"They wouldn't be going to the library, exactly," said Teddy. "I just assume that, if they think they have only a short time before we go searching down there, they may make a desperate attempt to move the treasure elsewhere, before we find it. And that's when we'll catch them."

"Oh," said Gorilla, "I see." He breathed deeply and scowled. "Couldn't we just tell them that we found the treasure, and now the game's over, so whoever took it can tell us and we'll all have a good laugh?"

"You did agree to rely on my expertise here," said Teddy. "Please, let's try it my way."

"But," Gorilla continued, his scowl deepening, "if we tell them we're going to go down later in the day and then go down immediately . . . well, wouldn't that be a lie too?"

Teddy sighed. "It could be, but I'll phrase it so it isn't. Anyway, even if we go down immediately, that's still later in the day, if you see what I mean. But, you see, old fellow, that's the nature of wickedness. When people behave wickedly, you sometimes have to leave them to deceive themselves . . . if you see what I mean."

Gorilla nodded vigorously. "I haven't the foggiest idea what you mean," he said.

"Gor-Gor," said Porculina fondly, "you're so . . . apey."

"You understand him, then?" asked Gorilla.

"Oh, not at all," said Porculina shaking her head, "but I don't have to. I'm just the slow-witted sidekick in this story. All I have to do is say something like, 'By George, old bear, that's a capital plan!' And then maybe something like, 'Right, old chap, we'll conceal ourselves in the darkness and when the thieves show themselves we'll pounce on them and capture them in a clever device built from cardboard boxes, wooden boards, ropes, string, hot-chocolate mugs, and toothbrushes!' Then Teddy will say something like . . ." She turned to Teddy expectantly.

"Oh, ah, yes, right," said the little bear. He cleared his throat, and in his best professional's voice, added, "That's not exactly how I have it planned, my dear old pig, as I shall explain presently. But you have the general gist of it." He smiled. "Was that all right?"

"Perfect," said Porculina.

At that moment, Rolandus approached the table. "Excuse me, miss, sirs," he said, "but I slipped out and listened to the battery-powered wireless a few moments ago, and I think the roads will be cleared by morning. Electricity should be restored sometime today also, and phone lines too."

"Really?" asked Gorilla. "Oh, that's a pity. That means some of my guests will be leaving."

"Alas, sir," Rolandus replied, "that is the way of things."

"That also means the police can be called," said Porculina. "We simply can't let them elbow in on our mystery, Teddykins. We have to solve the thing before they get here."

"And just a moment ago you were complaining that everything was moving along at too fast a clip," said Teddy with a smile. Then, in a slightly graver tone, he added, "But it also means that the thieves may be able to get away before we've caught them. So, I agree with you, Pigsy. We have to set our trap now. Rolandus," he said, turning his eyes to the butler, "could you perhaps sit down with us so that I can tell you something?"

"Ah, no, sir," Rolandus answered, "I very much fear I could not. It's not quite the thing, you see . . . not done."

"Oh, stuff and nonsense," said Gorilla, "that's silly. Just pull up a chair and sit down, Roly."

"No, sir, really, I couldn't . . ."

"Oh, please, Roly," said Gorilla in an imploring tone, "please please please, oh please please . . ."

"Yes, yes, sir," said Rolandus, raising his paws before him and glancing to either side apprehensively, "as you say, sir." He looked about him a little uncomfortably.

All the other guests were absorbed in conversations of their own, however, except for Cuttles, who was staring off into the distance and talking quietly to himself ("Oh, cruel fate!" he could be heard saying. "Cast up upon this bleak, barren shore, with but this piece of dry toast for company . . . . Yes, that's very good.").

Rolandus fetched a chair from another table and rather stiffly seated himself. "Now, sir, what did you wish to speak to me about?"

"Whatever I tell you," Teddy said, "please keep your composure."

Rolandus arched an eyebrow. "I always do."

"Yes, of course," said Teddy. Then, quietly but urgently, he narrated the events of the morning for Rolandus. The dog's face betrayed surprise as the tale unfolded — the hidden door, the secret library, the flooding cistern — and by its end there was a distinct look of alarm in his eyes, but he made no noise or movement that would have alerted the other guests. When Teddy finished, Rolandus sat for several moments in silence, and then at last remarked, "I must say, sir, that I am genuinely . . . astonished."

"Aren't we all?" said Porculina.

"But there's more," said Teddy, "and we'll need your help now, and Woof's too, if you'd be so kind as to take him aside and tell him the story I just told you. First, though, I'll need you to ask the guests and the staff to gather in that sitting room just next to the treasure room in about half an hour. Tell them nothing else. You see, we're going to lay a trap . . ."

CHAPTER 11

The Trap Is Sprung

"YOU KNOW," SAID GORILLA TO TEDDY A LITTLE more than half an hour later, "I've a wonderful idea. Why don't you come here and live at the castle with me? I mean, when you're not traveling? Make this your base of operations, as it were? It would be so jolly. You don't have to worry about nationality or papers or passports, of course, since international law says soft toys are citizens of the whole world. Oh, please come, please please . . ."

The two of them were standing by a window in the sitting room, with Porculina only a few feet away, while all the guests and servants were settling themselves. Rolandus was going about thanking various of the toys for coming and asking whether they were in need of anything. Blue Bunny wore a large white bandage around his head, rather like the one Gorilla had worn in the morning, but with his ears sticking out through the gauze; otherwise he seemed his usual alert and quivery self. Miss Raccoon was sitting beside him, smiling sympathetically and speaking to him softly. Cuttles, who was more or less heaped into a deep armchair, was sighing rather loudly, and occasionally could be overheard working on one of his dramatic monologues ("Ah, Fate, so cruel, remorseless, and dark — Fate that has cast me snowbound into this bitter fastness, so shadowy, forbidding, and desolate, with naught but hard stone walls and ice-cold armchairs . . ."). Woof and Mr MacAw were speaking to one another from their chairs by a tea table, the pandas were standing silently by the large open entranceway to the foyer, and the frogs were comfortably seated on a divan and chatting.

"That's very good of you," said Teddy to Gorilla. "The idea is very appealing, I have to say."

Just then, Rolandus approached them. "I think all is in readiness," he said. "Shall I call things to order?"

"Allow me," said Teddy, stepping away from the window and raising his paws. "Excuse me, ladies and gentletoys," he called out, "excuse me."

The murmur of voices subsided.

"Thank you all so much for allowing us to impose on you. We have some news to impart, some of it quite important, and it seemed best to bring you all together here at one time. First of all, you will no doubt be relieved to learn that Mr Rolandus anticipates a restoration of electricity and phone service shortly, and that the roads are in the process of being cleared."

A dulcet hum of pleased voices rippled around the room for a moment.

"But the more important reason for calling you here," Teddy continued, pausing for a moment for dramatic effect, "is that there's been a development in the mystery of the missing treasure."

"Goodness," said Miss Raccoon, "how exciting."

Blue Bunny leaned forward, his nose twitching furiously. "Wonderful, sir, wonderful!" he cried in his high, carroty voice. "Does that mean you know who attacked me, sir? And the Laird too, of course? Does it, sir? This is wonderful indeed! Oh, dear, I almost feel faint." And indeed he looked as though he were a little dizzy from his excitement.

"No," said Teddy, "but we soon shall know. Please be calm, Mr Bunny. You all remember that secret passage I told you about at breakfast?"

"No," said Mr MacAw in a tone of withering sarcasm, "we've forgotten entirely."

Teddy smiled. "Yes, yes," he said, "all right. It was only a rhetorical question. Anyway, we've discovered a second secret door, situated *within* the passage. It leads to a flight of stairs that appears to lead down some considerable depth into the castle, or even beneath it."

There were several exclamations of surprise.

"Och, weel, that's certainly a page-turner," said Ribbit. "Is that where ye think yer thieves got to, then?"

"Undoubtedly," said Teddy.

"Let's go after them!" cried Jumping Bean delightedly, hopping down from the divan.

"Not so quickly," said Teddy. "Anyway, it's unlikely the thieves are there now. You've got the right idea, though. We do indeed need to investigate thoroughly. Several of us will be going down later today, I assure you."

"Goodness," said Miss Raccoon, "how daring!" And she fluttered her eyelashes fetchingly. "Especially on your part, Teddy."

Teddy swallowed and straightened his tie (which was already quite straight). "Well . . . well . . . well, that's very kind of you to say. It's . . . well, it's all part of standard police work, you know . . ."

"Teddykins won't be alone," interjected Porculina impatiently.

"Yes, I'm coming too," said Jumping Bean.

"Nay, ye're not," said his uncle sternly. "That's nae job for a wee taddie."

141

"And what precisely," Cuttles suddenly said in a mournful tone, "do you hope to find?"

Teddy was surprised by the question but answered politely. "The treasure, ideally, or the thieves, or both, or at least some evidence regarding who the thieves . . ."

"I don't refer to what you hope to discover," the squid interrupted, "but to what you hope to *find*."

"Umm," said Porculina with narrowing eyes, "what's the difference, exactly?"

"I mean to say, do you imagine that, whatever you may or may not *discover*, you will *find* happiness as a result? Do you delude yourself that happiness is to be *found* at the end of this . . . this sordid little intrigue that fate has arranged for us?"

"Well . . ." Teddy glanced around the room, momentarily at a loss for words. "Well, we're not really searching for happiness as such — not just at the moment."

"Ah," said Cuttles meaningfully, "just so. There, at least, you show wisdom."

Woof rolled his eyes. "Aye, weel, good t' get that cleared up. So, then, what's the plan?"

"You know," said Gorilla, "I rather do expect to find happiness at the end of the story. I generally do. I say, who's up for a pirate adventure?"

"Wait," said Teddy, "let's hold off on that for now, please. And thank you, Jumping Bean, but the search party has already been determined. I shall go with Rolandus, Porculina, and the Laird."

"Do you think, however," said Cuttles, "that, before you go, his Lairdship might grace us all with some music? Just so as to smooth our furrowed brows, and to soothe our angry souls, and to make sweet the drowsy afternoon? Some of that divine bagpipes music of which he gave us all too brief a sample last night, perhaps? I've been hankering for it so."

The rest of the guests and staff issued a variety of low soft noises that, in combination, made it seem almost as if the walls were moaning in pain.

"Oh, ah, goodness," Miss Raccoon remarked.

"Aye, weel," said Ribbit, and then fell silent.

"Oh, you see," said Teddy, "you see — you see — yes. No, you see, well, we simply must get on with our explorations. There's so much to . . . see . . . and — "

A chorus of grateful voices suddenly drowned out his words with abnormally loud exclamations of "Yes, of course!" and "We quite understand!" and "Time is of the essence!"

Cuttles looked about rather disconsolately, limply waved a couple of tentacles before him, and said, "Surely there's no absolutely immediate . . . "

But now there was a positive eruption of voices on all sides, crying out things like "Oh, no, we mustn't delay them!" and "There's no time!" and "The thieves will get away!"

Cuttles dropped his tentacles, looked around, breathed deeply, and said, "Very well, I see I'm overborne in this matter. I defer to the opinion of . . . the mob."

"Quite right," said Gorilla. "I'd love to play the bagpipes for you, but that will just have to wait till after dinner."

"Speaking of which," said Pandus, stepping forward from the doorway, "preparations will have to begin shortly if we're to have tea ready and then to serve dinner on time. Is there, ah, any further need of us just now?"

"Oh, what will you be serving at teatime?" Porculina asked. "Will there be any of those glorious banana-ginger biscuits I've heard so much about?"

Pandus looked at her impassively. "Yes, I believe so. Banana cake as well. And there'll be banana, ginger, and nutmeg soup at dinner, as well as banana tart in cherry sauce. Indeed, miss, I can honestly say that there is scarcely a banana-based dish that will not be laid before you during your sojourn here. It's" — he shrugged, almost sadly — "the specialty of the house, *la spécialité de la maison*, as it were."

Mr MacAw clapped his beak together a few times, and then said, "I have to admit that, when all's said and done, I don't really fancy banana quite as much as all that."

"Aye," said Ribbit, "neither do I."

"Though, of course," the parrot added, remembering himself, "what I mean to say is that, while I'm not overly fond of bananas as such, your gifts as a chef make everything you serve utterly delightful."

"True, true," said Ribbit hastily, also recalling his manners, "and nae one could say otherwise."

Pandus said nothing, but merely looked at each of them gravely for a moment, and then politely gave a slight bow of his head. He turned to Gorilla. "With your permission, milord, we'll go down to the kitchens."

Gorilla, however, was clearly distracted. He was turning his head back and forth slowly, staring now at Mr MacAw and now at Ribbit with an expression of deep worry, and slowly wringing his hands before him.

"Milord?" Pandus said again.

"What? Yes?" Gorilla looked at his chef. "Oh, yes, of course, old chap. Please."

The pandas departed.

"Right," said Teddy a moment later, "so we'll go ahead with our investigation, then. I suppose . . . well, would you say we might need some supplies, Mr Rolandus?"

The dog nodded thoughtfully. "It would perhaps be prudent."

"Right," said Porculina firmly, striding forward and adopting her sidekick intonations, "that's the thing. Let's see, old bear, just the necessaries, then: ropes, flares, flashlights, snowshoes, mountain-climbing boots, scuba-diving equipment, radios, and lollipops. Do you think you have all of that up in the . . . um, in the attic, Mr Rolandus?"

Rolandus's posture became a little stiffer. "Ah, well . . . some of those items, miss."

"Look, let's go," said Teddy suddenly, "and leave everyone else alone right now. We'll report our findings later." And, pausing only to smile winningly at the other guests, albeit a little nervously at Miss Raccoon, he hurriedly urged Gorilla, Porculina, and Rolandus towards the door.

"Before ye go," Woof said, "is it all reet if I steal Blue here away t' help me try to fix that generator — just in case the electricity is slow in coming on? What d'ye say t' that, auld cony?"

"What?" said the Rabbit. "Oh, I'm not sure." He turned his twitching snout rapidly in all directions. "What with my . . ." He pointed to the bandage about his head.

"Aye, weel, I'll be gentle on you," said Woof. "I only need ye to hold m' torch and tell me where some things are kept."

"Ah, but . . ."

"Go on, Blue," said Rolandus. "I have to help the Laird and his friends, and you know the ins and outs down there."

Blue Bunny placed a paw on his head, gently felt about the edges of his bandages, quivered anxiously a few times, and then flashed a slightly frantic smile. "Yes, indeed, of course, absolutely, sirs and ma'ams. We can stop by the kitchen and get some biscuits and carrots and things, can't we? I'm famished and I don't know how long . . ."

"Aye, o' course," said Woof. "Truth be told, even wi' that fine lunch in me, I'm a wee bit hungry m'self."

*   *   *

When Teddy, Porculina, Gorilla, and Rolandus had passed through the foyer and walked around the far side of the great staircase, Teddy gestured for the others to stop and beckoned them aside into the passage leading to the service stairs.

"We'll wait for the others to clear out," he said, "and then head right back into the treasure room." He frowned. "I wish Woof hadn't asked for Blue's help just then, though. I expect he thinks that Blue isn't under any suspicion, because of that crack he took on the head last night, but I'd prefer everyone were left unattended for the nonce. Now, you see, Gorilla," — he turned to his friend — "I didn't positively say we were actually going to go and collect supplies. I merely asked . . ." But he stopped because he could see that Gorilla was not really listening. "What's on your mind, old fellow?"

Gorilla lifted his eyes, which now had a brooding and perhaps despairing look in them. "It doesn't matter, does it?" he said gravely. "We don't need to set a trap now. We know who the criminals are." He shook his head sadly.

"What?" said Teddy. "Who? Who do you mean?"

"*Whom*," corrected Porculina.

"Isn't it obvious?" said Gorilla, now gazing at the floor. "Why, it's Alasdair and Ribbit, of course."

"What makes you say that?" asked Porculina.

Gorilla looked at each of the others in turn and then shook his head in disbelief. "Didn't you hear them? Both of them said they disliked ... bananas. Horrible, horrible ... horrible. Obviously there's something deeply wrong with them, at a level we can't comprehend."

"Now, wait ..." Teddy began.

"Don't you see?" Gorilla persisted. "They may be mad — criminally mad. They may imagine themselves to be anything. Anyone who would turn against bananas ..."

"No, no, you can't ..." Teddy began.

"He may be right," said Porculina suddenly. "Cream-puffs and persimmons! I mean, why would anyone say he doesn't like bananas? Maybe they really are — well, a little warped." Then she gasped. "Oh, I've got it! Maybe they're part of some strange criminal cult that's taken some sort of vow not to eat bananas, and another vow to rob all the castles of Scotland using ... oh, maybe druidical magic or something ... or just using hidden passages that they know about because, in their dark banana-hating mad subtlety, they've managed to gather all the ancient maps and journals and ..." She paused, however, because Teddy was staring at her quizzically.

"Um," said the little bear after a moment, "are you, uh, you know ... playing the part of the slow-witted sidekick right now ... or ...?"

Porculina bit her lower lip, glancing at Gorilla and then Rolandus. "Why?" she said. "Should I be?"

146   Teddy said nothing.

She cleared her throat, looked about uncertainly again, and then all at once assumed a bold expression. "Well, yes ... of course ... *yes*, of course, that's exactly what I was doing ... um, my dear old bear. Ho ho ho. Ho." She smiled wanly. "Ho?"

"If you'll excuse me, miss, sirs," said Rolandus, who had just been cautiously peering out of the corridor and through the balustrade at the staircase's lower steps, "but I believe the coast is clear, as they say."

"Good," said Teddy, relieved to change the subject. "Did you manage to get that thing I asked for?" he asked Rolandus.

"The broom handle?" replied the dog. "Yes, sir, it's waiting by the door to the secret corridor."

"What do you want that for, Teddykins?" asked Porculina.

But Teddy merely held a finger to his lips and motioned for the others to come along.

*　　*　　*

"Gor-Gor," Porculina whispered sharply across the dimly lit library from her hiding-place under the desk, "you simply must stop making little train noises."

"It's not a train," Gorilla whispered back from behind an armchair, "it's a steamboat, with a large paddle-wheel, going down the Mississippi ... "

"Even so," said Porculina, "we have to remain absolutely silent."

"Oh, all right," said Gorilla. But then, a few moments later, his voice began faintly to float across the open space again: "*Chunga-chunga-chunga-chunga* ... "

"Oh, Gor-Gor, please!" Porculina whispered, even more sharply, and now with an additional note of pleading. "We can still hear you. You're going to ruin everything."

"Sorry," said Gorilla. "Still, I don't know why we're bothering with all this hiding. We know who the thieves are."

Teddy, who was crouched behind another armchair, sighed softly. "Gorilla, old ape," he whispered, "once again, not liking bananas is not a sign of wickedness or criminal insanity. Not all toys are the same. Not all have the same sense of taste or the same preferences. It doesn't mean anything. So, please, as Pigsy says, let's just try to stay silent and wait."

"Yes, all right," Gorilla said. "You explained all of that on the way down here." He said nothing for several seconds; then: "Still, it seems . . ."

"No, there's no 'still' about it," Teddy said. "Please, believe me, old friend."

"Oh . . . right-ho. So, then . . . everything all right, Roly?"

Rolandus, pressed into the shadows beside a large bookcase, quietly coughed. "Quite all right, sir," he whispered, "if a little dusty."

"Shhhhh . . ." said Teddy and Porculina both.

The four had been waiting at their various stations for nearly twenty minutes now. Teddy had told the others that, if the thieves were to come, they would surely come within the hour, thinking there was only a short time before the treasure would be discovered. Now he was beginning to wonder whether his stratagem had failed. The estimate of an hour had probably been too generous; the thieves, he believed, would come soon or not at all (and he was beginning to doubt it would be soon). He ran his finger along the plain wooden broom handle lying on the carpet beside him and dropped his chin in resignation.

But just then the distant but instantly recognizable sound of a great brick-and-mortar door opening at the top of one of the staircases gently pulsed through the room. Gorilla stood up and cupped his hands around his mouth, ready to call out, but Teddy was already on his feet motioning his friend to be silent and to get back out of sight. Gorilla, looking a little abashed, smiled, gently tapped the side of his own head with two fingers, and slipped down again behind the chair.

After a moment, there were further sounds: light and furtive footfalls on the steps, echoing softly in the enclosed space, and then the clear sound of anxious and labored breaths. After another moment, it became obvious that the sounds were coming from the stairs situated two entrances to the left from where the search party had entered the library. Whoever was coming was now only seconds away.

Teddy glanced over the arm of his chair and saw Rolandus drawing himself even deeper into the shadows beside the bookcase, which was set just to the right of the entrance from which the sounds were coming. Porculina and Gorilla were entirely hidden. Then, all at once, a largish figure came into view, at first just a shapeless shadow in the mouth of the enclosed staircase, and then a distinct form and face and attire, gently but clearly illumined by the gentle wintry light that fell from the ceiling window high above.

Teddy briefly pursed his lips and morosely shook his head. "I'd hoped I was wrong," he said to himself, so quietly that even he could not quite hear it.

As Teddy continued to watch, the figure hesitantly stepped into the room, obviously waiting to get accustomed to the pale light down here, and then took a few steps forward. At this, Rolandus quietly and gracefully slipped away from the bookcase, stepped behind the figure, straightened himself, clasped his paws behind his back, and said in a clear voice, "Very well, Chef, that will do."

Immediately Pandus spun around, both his hands flying up to the high toque on his head. "What?" he gasped. "Why . . . ? How . . . ?"

"I must say I'm deeply disappointed," said Rolandus with a certain stern dignity. "I would never have suspected you of this."

"I would have," said Teddy as he rose from his hiding place and stepped out into the open, broom handle in paw. "I regret to say it, but I had already begun to think you were involved."

Pandus turned, a frantic look on his normally somber face. "Now, sir, please don't imagine . . ."

"Oh, hullo, Pandus," Gorilla called out, standing up and leaning on the back of his armchair. "What are you doing here? Silly fellow, we were waiting to capture the thief. Now you've probably scared him away. I say, is tea ready?"

"Oh, Gor-Gor," said Porculina impatiently, crawling out from under the desk, standing up, and brushing herself off, "don't you see? Pandus is the thief. That's why he's here."

"Oh, nonsense," said Gorilla with a laugh, stepping out from behind his chair and waving his hand dismissively. "Really, old girl, you come up with the silliest things sometimes. Pandus couldn't possibly be a thief. If you'd only ever tasted his banana-ginger biscuits, you'd know; no one who could bake anything that wonderful could possibly want to steal any silly old bits of gold and such."

Pandus said nothing. He merely looked at his employer with an expression somewhere between anxiety and sorrow and then lowered his eyes.

"No," said Teddy, "I'm sorry, old fellow, but Porculina is right. Mr Pandus here, brilliant chef though he is, is also undoubtedly our culprit. Or, rather, one of our culprits."

Gorilla's brow furrowed. "Now, Teddy, if I didn't know better, I'd think you were accusing Pandus of robbery."

"I am," said Teddy. "That's exactly what I'm doing. Pandus is a robber. He stole your treasure."

Gorilla stared at Teddy, then at Pandus, then at Teddy again, and gently bit his lower lip for a moment. "I'm not following you at all, old fellow. It almost sounds as if you're accusing Pandus here of a crime."

"Oh, golly-gosh," said Porculina. "This isn't nearly as thrilling as I thought it would be. It's actually a bit depressing. Everything was so nice before we knew who the thief was." She clenched her jaws for a moment in distaste. "Oh, well, if it has to be done . . ." She took three steps towards Pandus, narrowed her eyes, crouched slightly, almost like a wrestler about to pounce, thrust a trotter forward, and cried out in a voice of fierce triumph, "Ho ho, my good fellow, you thought you could escape justice, but justice is the swiftest thing of all!"

For a moment, no one said anything. Pandus merely stared at Porculina with an expression of mild surprise.

Porculina straightened up, breathed deeply, and said, "Perhaps I didn't do it right." She closed her eyes for a moment, her trotters drawn together before her face. Then she opened her eyes again, squinted even more menacingly at Pandus, and said, in a calmer but more sinister voice,

"Ho ho, my good fellow, you thought you could escape justice, but justice is the swiftest thing of all!"

At first, Pandus again failed to react; after a moment, however, he seemed to grasp what was expected of him. "Oh! Oh, yes, of course. Yes, miss, very terrifying. I am most suitably chastened."

Gorilla approached the panda, but was still looking at Teddy. "Now, let me get this straight. Are you implying . . . "

"Yes," said Teddy, "yes, I'm afraid we are."

"I say, Pandus old chap, did you really take that silly treasure? And did you *thonk* me on the head in the maze?"

"Salty ice-cream, that's right!' Porculina suddenly cried out. "Was that you, then? Were you the dastardly villain who viciously attacked this . . . noble ape? Oh, that was a foul deed!"

Pandus looked from Porculina to Gorilla, obviously ashamed of himself. "Yes, that was I," he said. "I was the one who bonked the Laird on the head with . . . "

"No, it was a *thonk*," said Gorilla, "a distinct *thonk*."

"Oh, was it?" said Pandus listlessly. "I'm sorry, it was meant to be a bonk. Anyway, I didn't expect it would do any harm. I only used a long-stemmed white lily. I'd grabbed one from the treasure room on the way out, and I hit you with it purely out of desperation. I didn't expect it to work, though. I didn't even hit you hard. I certainly didn't think I could knock you out. But then you . . . well, you just lay down and began snoring, and so . . . " His voice trailed off.

"A . . . lily?" said Porculina. "It was just a . . . *lily*?" She looked at Gorilla. "But, Gor-Gor, I was so worried about you. A lily?"

"Now, now," said Gorilla, raising a forefinger, "you were the one who insisted that a *thonk* is a *thonk* is a *thonk*."

"Yes, but . . . " began Porculina.

"And what would you do if you were *thonked* on the noggin in a moonlit maze in the middle of an exciting mystery? Surely you'd know to slump to the ground and lose consciousness."

"Yes, well," said the little pig in a perplexed tone, "I suppose that's true."

"Where does that stairway lead?" asked Teddy.

"Oh," — Pandus glanced over his shoulder — "just up to the larder. There's a secret door behind our stores of bamboo in the alcove."

"And how did you find that door? By chance? Or did someone show it to you?"

Pandus straightened his shoulders. "I prefer not to say, sir."

"Oh, come now," said Rolandus, somewhat gruffly, "the game's up, surely you can see that. Who was your accomplice? It'll be better for everyone if you speak up now."

Pandus said nothing.

"Was it . . ." the dog continued, "was it . . . Panda?"

The chef wheeled about and stared appalled at Rolandus. "No, of course not. How could you say such a thing? In fact, the thing I fear most right now is her disappointment in me when she hears of this."

"Well, who then?" said Teddy. "There's no way you could have moved all that treasure by yourself."

"Please, sir," said Pandus, turning back to the bear, "permit me the dignity of not betraying a friend."

"Well, if you ask me," said Porculina, "you already did that when you stole from this fine, gentle, generous ape here."

Pandus dropped his gaze to his feet. "Yes, miss, that's true, I know. Permit me the dignity of not betraying yet *another* friend, then."

"We can't, I'm afraid," said Teddy. "Still, we don't have to insist on the point just now. So, if you'll excuse me . . . this won't hurt a bit . . ." And, with that, he stepped a little closer, extended the broom handle, and gently tapped the panda on the shoulder with it. "Chef Pandus," he said in a clear officious voice, "I do arrest thee of theft and of . . . ah, treason against thy liege."

The panda drew back slightly. "What's that you say?"

"Oh, I just mean you're under arrest for stealing," said Teddy. "Sorry, I was trying to be traditional about it, what with this being Britain, and my using a pole in the traditional fashion, and this being a castle . . ."

"Pole?" said Pandus. "What does a pole signify?"

"Don't you know?" said the bear. "It's a very ancient custom. When a policeman touches you with his pole, then you're bound over by law, which means you're honor-bound to surrender and not to attempt escape."

"Really?" said Pandus.

"Really?" said Gorilla, Porculina, and Rolandus in unison.

"Yes, really," said Teddy. "And though there are of course human criminals who would ignore the rules and make a break for liberty, it would be far, far below the standards of a soft toy to ignore the dictates of honor."

"Oh," said Pandus, looking over his shoulder again towards the stairs. "But, sir, this is very vexing . . . and very inconvenient! I wish you had warned me. I was, in fact, intending to make a break for it. I was just going to point towards that corner over there and yell, 'Look! A hippopotamus!' and then, when you all turned to look, I was going to dash madly for the stairs and up through the kitchen, lock the door behind me, and run wildly out through the snow in a vain attempt to get away. I expect I would have collapsed somewhere near the rose bushes, sobbing with shame and fatigue."

"I thought you might be thinking of that," said Teddy, "but now you can't do it. I'm sorry, but there it is. Honor is a soft toy's very essence."

"Well," said Pandus, "as I say, that's very inconvenient. What a vexation."

"I'm sorry, old fellow," said Gorilla, "but I just don't see what hippopotamus you're talking about."

"Let's all go up now," Teddy said. "I think we can tie this matter up fairly easily now."

So they all ascended the stairs leading to the secret corridor and the treasure room, Porculina leading the way, followed by Rolandus, then Pandus, then Teddy, and finally Gorilla, who paused only long enough to take another good look at the corner where Pandus had pointed and to shake his head in consternation.

153

Just as they had reached the treasure room, there was a sudden flickering of yellow brightness along the walls and three electric lamps came on.

"Oh, good," said Teddy, "just in time to cast a little light on the matter. Rolandus, could you gather everyone once more in the sitting room there? It's time we see if we can bring an end to this mystery once and for all."

CHAPTER 12
All Is Revealed

THE MOOD IN THE SITTING ROOM WAS DISTINCTLY somber. The snow-pale daylight coming in through the broad double window gave everything a kind of mild frosty clarity. Only two small electric lamps were lit, back in the room's deeper recesses.

Pandus, standing by the closed door to the treasure room, was gazing morosely away towards the window, having just confirmed with a few wordless, sullen nods the story Teddy had told the assembled guests and staff. Mr MacAw sat in his high-backed armchair with folded wings and a look of austere disapproval in his eyes. Panda was now seated on the divan wringing her paws anxiously, with Miss Raccoon seated beside her and speaking to her gently. Woof and Ribbit, both standing near the doorway leading to the foyer, were shaking their heads and exchanging quiet words, while Jumping Bean gazed at the disgraced chef grimly. Blue Bunny, no longer wearing the bandage on his head, had an expression of pure dismay on his face as he sat on a sofa near the middle of the room, twitching his nose and scratching his ears. Gorilla was sitting on the arm of a sofa with his head in his hands and Porculina was standing beside him with a comforting trotter on his shoulder. Rolandus, standing a few paces away from Pandus, was composed but clearly displeased. And Cuttles, sitting somewhat apart in a chair on the other side of a large marble-topped coffee table, seemed his normal, melancholy self.

"So," said Teddy, "the problem remains. Clearly Mr Pandus had one accomplice, and maybe more, and — barring the discovery of someone hidden in a cupboard or under the stairs — we have to consider the possibility that someone here . . . "

"Oh, dear," said Miss Raccoon, "surely there's not still a cloud of suspicion hovering over us?"

"I assume," Mr MacAw suddenly squawked, "that you're accusing me!"

"What?" said Teddy in genuine surprise. "No. Why do you say that?"

"Isn't it obvious?" the parrot said sharply. "Parrots have exceptional hearing, and as I was going up the stairs after our last little conference here, I distinctly heard the Laird saying that my tepid feelings in regard to bananas clearly marked me out as a . . . "

"Oh, no, no, no!" Teddy interrupted. "Gorilla was simply confused on a point of criminal psychology. But that's all been cleared up. He no longer suspects . . . "

"Well, I absolutely adore bananas," said Miss Raccoon with a radiant smile.

Just then Gorilla gave out a soft sad groan. "Oh, Pandus, how could you?" he said, not lifting his head from his hands. "How could anyone who makes such splendid food be a thief? I don't know what to think any more."

"Perhaps," Cuttles said, "I can put the matter somewhat more . . . poignantly. I've been thinking of a monologue that might give poetical expression to the grief we all share. If I may —" He lifted up four tentacles, looked up to the ceiling, gave vent to a moan so ghastly that everyone else in the room flinched in terror (Blue Bunny actually gave out a yelp), and began to intone loudly: "Ah, woe! Ah dismal, pitiless woe! Ah, woeful woe!" There he paused, however, as if considering. "No, that may be a bit too much woe. Let's see: Ah, woe, that so dark a fate should here befall! Oh, how — how, I say, how — could one so gifted, so rich in joys imparted, turn his hand to evil works, to works of darkness and . . . umm, woe . . . ?" He fell silent with a look of uncertainty in his great golden eyes.

"Oh, oh, can I try?" said Porculina, stepping away from Gorilla and into the middle of the room.

Cuttles gave a courtly nod.

"Right," said Porculina, clearing her throat. All at once, a look of anguish came into her eyes, she raised her clasped trotters high before her, gazed upward, and cried out, "Oh, Chef — Chef! — artist of such transcendent prowess, master of the most exquisite culinary arts, how canst thou have turned thy noble hand to deeds of such grievous perfidy? How, when thy soups, thy custards and parfaits, would seem to proclaim a soul of the most exquisite delicacy? How . . ."

Cuttles coughed meaningfully and cut her off. "Yes, yes, very good, especially for a first attempt. But I think you need to give it a bit more tragic grandeur. Perhaps if you were to set the mood with an initial 'Woe!' or 'Oh, cruel fate!' or maybe . . ."

"Please," said Teddy, "we really should concentrate on the matter of . . ."

But now Gorilla interrupted. Seeming to have forgotten his misery of only moments before, he had risen from the sofa's arm, clapped his hands together, and begun bouncing lightly on the tips of his toes. "Oh, oh, let me have a go! Please. Let's see . . . umm . . . Oh, woe! Woe! Oh, woe . . . umm, whoa there . . . whoa, horsey!"

"No, no . . ." Porculina began.

157

"Please," Teddy said again, "there'll be time for all of this later."

"Och," said Woof, "this is gettin' beyond me. Why doesn't Pandus jus' tell us who his confederates were. C'mon auld whiskers, the jig's up. Best t' make a clean breast of it."

But Pandus said nothing.

"All right," said Teddy, "let's recount the events of last night, and see if we can make any sense of them."

"Maybe we can reenact them," Porculina said eagerly.

"I say, that would be fun," Gorilla said.

"I think it would also take more time than we really have," said Teddy. But then, seeing their expressions of disappointment, he added, "Next time there's a mystery, we will, I promise. Just let me tell the tale for now."

And, in as few words as possible but omitting no significant detail, Teddy rehearsed the story of the previous night — the loss of electricity, the loud noise that had roused him and the others, the locked door, the undisturbed snow below the window, the discovery of Blue Bunny, the discovery of the secret corridor, the chase through the maze, the assault on Gorilla, and finally the loss of the snow-shoe tracks — while everyone else listened spellbound, as if hearing it all for the first time.

When Teddy had finished, the room remained silent for nearly a minute.

"Gosh!" said Porculina finally. "Meringue and melons! Crumblies! It all sounds so gripping when you repeat it. I mean, I was there, but you make it all come back so clearly."

"Yes, thanks," said Teddy. "I like to think I'm good at the summing up."

"In the darkness last night it was all so confusing. One thing just sort of merged into another. I don't know if I could have laid it out so well. But I have to say, here in the clear light of day, you can really see how all the different bits fit together ... one thing right after another ... just like in a mystery novel. I wish we'd had more light last night. Oh," — she turned to Woof and then to Blue Bunny — "I'm so glad you two were able to get the electricity back on. I wouldn't want to go through another night like that."

"Weel, truth t' be told," said Woof, "th' electricity came on quite wi'oot our help. The road crews oot there beat us to it, it seems. But we did manage to get the auxiliary generator fixed anyway. It'll work when it's needed next."

"What was amiss with it?" asked Rolandus.

"Aye, weel, there's the curious thing," said Woof. "It was a fairly simple matter, really. There was a wee grimpen in the wiggle-chute, and the gumption was a bit snazzled, and there was a wangled bit that jus' needed a wee bit of dewangling. To tell the truth, I'd almost think it was sabotage. I can't see how the problems could have been caused by accident. And I'm not sure why auld Blue couldna set things to rights last night, t' be honest. Were ye a mite distracted, auld cony?"

Blue Bunny suddenly realized that the question was addressed to him. "What?" he said in a shrill and agitated voice. "Why didn't I . . .? Well, it was so dark down there, of course. And there was so much on my mind. You know, I'm not really a very calm sort of rabbit." The pitch of his voice was rising steadily and his ears were shaking indignantly. "I know I'm not perfect at my job, but I try! There was so much I had to think about — the guests, seeing to the gates . . . umm . . . oh, and the lights going out, and the blizzard, and arranging for the van for carrying the treasure away, and helping prepare rooms for the unexpected guests, and getting the . . ."

"I'm sorry," Teddy interrupted, "what was that? What was that bit about a van for the treasure?"

Blue Bunny gazed frantically at the little bear and then, quite unexpectedly, gave out a scream of surprise.

"Goodness!" cried Miss Raccoon.

"Oh, it wasn't my van!" protested Blue Bunny. "It's the one his Lairdship wanted me to charter. Honestly."

"His Lairdship . . ." Teddy began.

Everyone in the room slowly turned to look at Gorilla.

"Gor-Gor," said Porculina gently, "what's this about a . . . van? For the treasure?"

Gorilla's face grew thoughtful for a moment and he sat down on the arm of the sofa again. "A van," he said softly, "a van . . . a van . . . . Oh, yes!" He stood up again. "Yes, that, of course. I'd clean forgot. I'd decided to send the treasure back with Alasdair to put it all in his museum after all, because he wanted it there so much. Well, almost all of it. I wasn't" — he turned to Mr MacAw with a slightly sheepish expression — "I wasn't going to send along that splendid paperclip necklace. I'm sorry. I mean, it's really the prize of the collection, and I didn't think it should leave the castle. But all the rest of it was going. The van was supposed to come tomorrow."

Mr MacAw was gazing at Gorilla in pure astonishment. "That's . . . that's extremely gracious of you, your Lairdship. But . . . but why didn't you mention it before now?"

Gorilla shrugged. "I expect I meant it as a surprise. Or perhaps I forgot. Or both. Anyway, it all comes back to me now."

"Ah, Gorilla," Teddy ventured, "whom exactly did you tell about this plan of yours?"

Gorilla turned to Teddy. "What plan?"

"The plan to send your treasure to Mr MacAw's museum?"

"Oh, that. I'm not sure. Does it matter?"

"It may. It may explain why the robbery took place so hurriedly, and under such unpromising circumstances. I mean, one of the strangest things about this robbery is that it occurred during a blizzard, when there was little hope of getting the bounty safely and quickly away. And then it was all done so clumsily."

"Well, then," said Gorilla, "let's see . . . Did I tell you, Roly, old boy?"

The dog shook his head. "No, sir. This is all news to me. And, frankly, I would have advised against such an undertaking."

"Would you have?" said Gorilla. "I say. Well, maybe I won't do it, then."

Mr MacAw's eyes widened and he shook his wings stiffly. "Now, your Lairdship, let's not be hasty here . . . "

"Oh, but, of course you didn't know, Roly," Gorilla continued, not noticing the parrot. "The idea came to me only after you'd left for Inverness to pick up Piggles and Teddy. And then when they got here I was too excited to remember anything about all that other boring business."

"Well, then," said Teddy, "whom did you tell?"

"That time you said 'whom,'" murmured Porculina.

Gorilla thought for another moment. "Just Blue, I suppose, when I asked him to arrange for it all."

Blue Bunny, leaping to his feet, screamed again, this time quite piercingly.

"Dear me!" exclaimed Miss Raccoon. "Please, Mr Bunny, I implore you!"

"I'm sorry, miss, really," he said in a frantic, chattering whine, "but everyone keeps making it sound like it was I who ... who ... oh ..." And he screamed again.

"Gracious!" said Ribbit. "Will ye get a grip on yerself, laddy?"

"Yes, calm yourself," said Teddy. "No one has accused you of anything yet."

"Oh, let him scream," Cuttles said indulgently. "We should probably all be screaming out against the pitilessness of fate, anyway. Don't you see there's a kind of horror in all of this—a kind of beautiful horror?"

"Would you care for a glass of water, Blue?" asked Rolandus, as if he had not heard Cuttles at all. "I was just going to check to see if the phone service had been restored, and I can quite easily bring you something."

Blue Bunny stared at the butler for a moment with a look of nervous gratitude on his quivering face and then settled back into his seat. "Oh, yes, Rolandus, yes, thank you, I am a bit thirsty ... and flustered."

"That's all right, Blue," said the dog, turning towards the entranceway to the foyer.

"I say, Roly old boy," Gorilla suddenly said, "I don't suppose you know where my big blue fuzzy blanket is—you know, the one with the snowflakes and caribou and whistles on it?"

"It's in a linen closet, sir," said Rolandus, "one quite nearby."

"Could you fetch it for me on the way, then?" said Gorilla. "It's a bit chilly in here."

161

"Yes, sir, of course," said the dog with a slight bow.

Once Rolandus had gone, Blue Bunny breathed deeply and said, somewhat more calmly, "I'm sorry for all the screaming. I do get nervous. Agitated, I suppose you'd say. Exercised. Anxious. A little . . . well, a little frazzled and bedazzled, as it were." His nose began twitching again. "It's just that, for a moment there, I thought Mr Teddy suspected me of being Pandus's accomplice."

"Oh, but I do," remarked Teddy casually.

Blue Bunny's ears stood straight up; his eyes became frighteningly wide; and then his head began to sway from side to side, as if he were about to faint. "Oh, sir," he said in a strangled but still shrill voice, "sir, sir, oh . . . sir . . . Why would you . . . sir . . . ?"

"Now, calm down, Blue," Teddy continued in an even tone. "Of course I suspect you. I mean, in a sense I suspect everyone, but in your case a pattern does seem to be emerging. Let's consider: First of all, the robbery was conducted at the worst possible time for a getaway, with every appearance of haste and poor planning. Why? The best explanation seems to be that the robbers knew that the treasure was to be sent away tomorrow, so were forced to make their move prematurely. Now, who knew that the treasure was being shifted? Other than Gorilla, only you. Second, we found you in the treasure room just after the robbery. You tell us you were knocked unconscious by the thieves, but how can we say if that's true? It's all but impossible to tell when a soft toy has taken a blow, unless a seam is split, and your seams are all quite intact. Third, Woof reports that the generator may have been sabotaged. Who went to work on it after the lights went out? You. So, did you go to fix the generator, or to disable it so as to make it harder for us to prosecute a proper investigation in good time? And, fourth, you stopped in at the kitchen on the way down to fix the generator with Woof, which you may have done in order to tell Pandus he was on his own moving the treasure to a new hiding place while we four were up in the attic getting supplies."

As Teddy had been speaking, Blue Bunny's expression had been becoming wilder and more hopeless, the trembling of his ears had been growing more violent, and little whimpers and gurgles of despair had been issuing with ever-greater frequency from his lips. But he said nothing.

"And, fifth of all," Teddy continued, now turning to Pandus, "how can you possibly claim that Blue Bunny was not your accomplice, Mr Chef, when he went to such trouble to help you move the treasure into the secret chamber downstairs last night? Why on earth would he have done that if he wasn't in league with you?"

Pandus looked shocked, and for a moment seemed to be struggling for words. He glanced about the room uncertainly. "Well, ah, well, sir," — he held out his open paws in a gesture of hapless ignorance — "perhaps he was only trying to be helpful. I mean, he's a very helpful . . ."

But his words were curtailed by Blue Bunny's shrillest shriek yet. "Oh, stop!" he cried, now on his feet again. "It's a trap, it's a trap! He's tricking you! Remember how cunning teddy bears are!"

Pandus fell silent, his eyes wide. "Oh, dear," he moaned, grabbing his toque from his head with both paws and hiding his face in it, "what have I done?"

"Now, really, sir," Blue Bunny cried, "you see he's confused! He didn't know what he was saying! He didn't understand! He . . . oh . . ." The rabbit opened his mouth to scream again, but all that came out now was a high thin whine, rather like the sound of steam from a distant kettle.

"I'm so sorry, Blue," Pandus said, still hiding his eyes. "I'm afraid they have us. Teddy Bears *are* so very cunning."

"No, they haven't got us!" the rabbit cried manically. "Everyone makes mistakes! Tell them you misspoke. They don't know — they weren't there when we stole the treasure and . . ." He paused, his eyes growing wide too, his tremulous paws rising to his mouth. "Oh, now what have *I* said?"

An excited murmur ran through the room. "Weel, weel, weel," Ribbit could be heard saying to his nephew. "My gracious goodness me," said Miss Raccoon, placing her dainty hands on either side of her lovely face.

163

"Extraordinary," remarked Mr MacAw. "Now falls a doom upon this noble house," Cuttles intoned softly off in the distance.

Suddenly, Blue Bunny flung his hands and ears high up above his head, looked directly into Pandus's eyes, and cried, "Run away, Pandus! Run away!" And he turned his shoulders as if he himself were about to make a dash for the window.

But Pandus somberly shook his head, lowered his toque from before his face, and said, "I'm sorry, Blue, but I can't. You see" — he shrugged — "Mr Bear has already touched me on the shoulder with a pole."

The rabbit became absolutely still for a moment, stared at the panda in obvious confusion, and then cried, "What? What does *that* mean?"

"Apparently," said Pandus, "it means I'm honor-bound not to run away."

Blue Bunny's nose twitched rapidly for several seconds; he glanced about the room several times and then returned his gaze to Pandus. "Well, could you perhaps just sort of *walk* away then . . . very vigorously?"

The chef looked at Teddy inquiringly, but the latter shook his head.

Pandus sighed and said, "I'm afraid that escape of any sort is out of the question."

"Are you all right, Blue?" Rolandus had just returned, and was standing in the entranceway with a glass of water in one hand and a large blue fluffy blanket in the other. "Here, take this." He crossed the room and held out the glass for the trembling rabbit.

Blue Bunny stared pathetically at the dog. Then, his features slowly relaxing into an expression of weakness and gratitude, he said, "It's all a mistake, honestly. A mistake." He took the water, raised it with shaking hands to his lips, and began to drink.

"As you requested, sir," said Rolandus, walking over to Gorilla and handing him the blanket.

"Oh, jolly good," said Gorilla, and immediately wrapped it about his shoulders.

"Oh, and one more thing," the dog added, returning to the entranceway, reaching around the jamb to the right, and retrieving a rather large gray burlap bag: "I found this in the linen closet, and wondered if anyone here had placed it there inadvertently."

Pandus looked at the sack, groaned, and buried his face in his toque again. At the same time, Blue Bunny turned his head sharply towards Rolandus, his nose twitching more furiously than ever; not thinking to right the angle of his glass, however, he emptied the remainder of his contents down his own chest.

"What's in it, exactly?" asked Teddy.

"Well," said Rolandus, opening the sack and staring down into it, "it contains a pair of snowshoes, a quantity of bamboo sprouts, two bunches of carrots, and this — " He reached down into the sack and withdrew a fairly large, obviously very old book, bound in dark green leather, and held shut with an ornate brass buckle.

"And what's that?" asked Porculina, advancing a step, a gleam of almost hungry curiosity in her eyes.

"It appears, miss, to be a bound volume of maps of the castle and its grounds, including a map of all its secret tunnels, in and out, which are quite numerous it seems, with instructions in the margins on how to find and open the various hidden doors. Oh, and inscribed on the flyleaf is a legend reading 'The Defenses of Castle MacGorilla, not to be removed from the guardhouse at any time.' Very curious. So, Blue," — the dog turned to the rabbit and stared at him with cold inquisitiveness — "how do you think this book, which obviously comes from some hiding place in the guardhouse where you live, might have got here?"

Blue Bunny dropped his glass to the floor, but the carpet prevented it from shattering. He swung his eyes about the room with a look of frantic terror. His nose, ears, fingertips, and toes were all now twitching rapidly and uncontrollably, and his limbs were shaking. Then he simply collapsed back onto the sofa in an attitude of utter defeat.

"Well," said Teddy grimly, "I think we've got the whole picture now. Blue Bunny found that book, approached Pandus, and they entered into a conspiracy to take the treasure. Am I right, Chef?"

Pandus nodded, but did not uncover his face. "We agreed on it some two months ago or more," he said softly.

Teddy looked at Porculina. "I believe there was something you wanted to say?"

Porculina looked as if she had just been shaken out of a daydream. "What? Oh, yes. Yes, I should jolly well say so." She knitted her brows, strode over to Blue Bunny, and took up a position directly in front of him with her trotters on her hips and her eyes smoldering with disapproval. "Bad bunny!" she said sharply. "Bad, bad bunny! Bad!"

Teddy cleared his throat. "Um, is that . . . all? Wasn't there something else?"

Porculina looked at him uncomprehendingly.

"You know, the other bit? The 'Ho, ho, my good fellow . . .'"

"Oh, that, of course," the little pig said. "How could I forget?" She turned back to Blue Bunny, straightened herself, swallowed deeply, and then fixed her eyes on him, an expression of icy triumph on her face. "Ho ho, my good fellow," she began, "you thought you could . . ."

But before she could say another word Blue Bunny shrieked, leapt to his feet, and bounded madly past her.

"Wait!" she cried, turning to call after him. "I'm not finished!"

But he was already past Teddy and Pandus too, and had reached the broad double window in three huge hops. He grabbed the sash of the left-hand window and yanked it upward. A rush of bitterly chilly air gusted into the room.

"Don't be a fool, ye daft auld cony!" Woof shouted at him.

Blue Bunny, still holding the window aloft, looked over his shoulder at everyone in the room. "I'm sorry, good toys," he whimpered shrilly. "I tried to be an honest rabbit. Truly I did. But it was all so much. I couldn't take it. My nerves, you see. So many responsibilities — opening gates, closing gates, wandering around the grounds . . . calling for vans . . . I hate telephones. They make so much noise. It was all so much. I needed to rest, you see . . . my cottage in the high hills . . ." He closed his eyes.

"Oh, my soul!" said Cuttles in an admiring voice. "How tragic! Bravo, Mr Bunny! Such pathos! But what will you do now?"

Blue Bunny opened his eyes again, and stared out of them desolately. "Well, sir," he whimpered, "I shall fly to the hills, become lost in the wild, crouch tremblingly amid the heather, forage like a wild ... monkey ..." — he winced — "... or ... or a savage turtle. I shall become an outlaw ... an outcast ... It's all I deserve. Listen for me henceforth only in the wailing of the cold and distant wind, sweeping over the barren crags and down the haunted valleys!" Then, stifling a sob, he turned and leapt headfirst through the window.

The dull, soft, curt sound of Blue Bunny's body striking the deep snow below the sill was audible throughout the room. So was the sound, a few moments later, of the rabbit's deeply muffled cry of alarm. So then was the sound, a few moments after that, of his muted but obviously frantic voice rising from the crystalline depths: "Hilpft! Oh, plizz ... Hrgmflpf! Hilpf! Igannot ... mooooovbf ...! Obe, plizzilpf!"

"Yes," said Rolandus with a hint of exasperation, "of course." He walked to the window and leaned out. Then, shaking his head, he straightened himself again and turned to Woof. "Do you think you might be able to assist me?" he asked. "Blue's feet are sticking up from the drift, and I think if each of us takes one, we just might be able to pull him out."

"Aye," said Woof, joining Rolandus. "It seems like a plan."

Both dogs leaned out of the window, reached down, and began to tug. Within a few moments, Blue Bunny could be heard sputtering shrilly, and then they had dragged him back into the room, covered with snow and shivering convulsively.

"All reet, auld cony," muttered Woof as they brushed the snow from the rabbit's ears and sides, "ye'll nae be tryin' that again, will ye?"

Blue Bunny merely sniveled softly.

Woof shook his head and went to lower the window sash.

"This way," Rolandus then said, and the dogs led the trembling rabbit back to the sofa and, gently but firmly, placed their paws upon his shoulders and pushed him down onto it.

Porculina strode forward again, her lips pursed in impatience. "Now, really," she said, "we'll have no more of . . ."

Blue Bunny suddenly lurched upward again, but this time he was unable to get all the way to his feet before the two dogs were pushing him down by the shoulders again.

"Hmmm," said Rolandus. "Ladies and gentletoys," he said, looking about the room, "I regret the measure I'm about to take, and I do ask you not to be disturbed." Then, looking down at Blue Bunny, he drew his lips back from his teeth and gave out a low but emphatic growl.

Not only Blue Bunny, but all the toys in the room stiffened for a moment.

"I say, Roly," said Gorilla a little nervously, "you're scaring the guests."

Rolandus resumed his normal mild expression. "I'm sorry, sir, but I needed Blue to sit still and to focus his mind. I think" — he looked down at the rabbit grimly — "I've made my point. Have I, Blue?"

Blue Bunny, eyes quite wide and ears drooping, nodded silently.

"Right, then," said Porculina, regaining her composure as well, "we can bring things to a close, then." Once again she assumed the cold look of triumph and cried, with a slightly metallic edge to her voice, "Ho ho, my good fellow, you thought you could escape justice, but justice is the swiftest thing of all!"

Blue moaned and dropped his eyes. "Yes," he said, "yes, it is."

"I say." Gorilla had set his blanket aside and was now approaching the sofa where the two dogs and Porculina were standing over the rabbit. "I'm beginning to get the impression that you all think Blue here was involved in this whole robbery business."

"But he was," said Porculina. "He's the other robber."

"Oh, I find that hard to believe," said Gorilla.

"But he just confessed . . . and tried to escape!"

"Still, let's not jump to conclusions."

"Really, old fellow," Teddy interjected, "she's right. Mr Bunny is definitely the culprit."

Gorilla's brow wrinkled. He turned to the rabbit. "Is this true, Blue?"

Blue Bunny gazed at Gorilla forlornly and then nodded his head.

Gorilla thrust out his lower lip. "I don't understand," he said sadly. "Pandus, Blue . . . I thought we were all friends here." He looked downward. "I'm confused. Doesn't everybody here . . ." — he peered at the two robbers in turn from under lowered brows, almost bashfully — " . . . love me?"

"Oh, Gor-Gor!" cried Porculina with deep feeling, rushing to Gorilla's side and placing a consoling trotter on his fine round head. "Of course, everybody loves you. How could they help it?"

"Milord," said Pandus, dropping his toque to the floor in his agitation, "please believe me, we both hold you in the highest esteem. We would not have betrayed you for the world, not in our right minds, but we were driven by . . . by sadness and desperation."

"Yes, sir," Blue Bunny's high carroty voice chimed in, "we . . . we . . . *revere* you. Oh, if only it weren't so hard!"

"So," said Gorilla, his head still turned down, "you do . . . *love* me?"

"Well, um," said Pandus, "not exactly how I'd put it, but yes, milord, I suppose that's how one *could* put it . . ."

"Yes, sir," added Blue, "of course, absolutely, utterly."

"Really?" asked Gorilla.

"Yes," both said.

"Really, truly?"

"Yes," both said again.

"Well, then," said Gorilla, instantly brightening, raising his head, and smiling, "that's all right then. I forgive you both. So," — he rubbed his hands together eagerly — "it's getting rather near teatime, isn't it. What's on board, Pandus old chap?"

"Now, wait," Porculina protested, putting her trotters on her hips, "you can't just forgive them like that. This is a mystery. And a crime's been committed. I mean . . . well, justice has to be done."

"Now, now," said Gorilla, wagging a finger, "haven't you ever heard that justice must be tampered with by Murphy?"

"Who?" said Porculina, scowling in confusion. "What?"

"I think he means," said Teddy, "that justice must be tempered by mercy."

"Oh," said Porculina. "Oh. Well, yes, but . . ." She looked at Gorilla. "Well, at least make them explain themselves."

"Blue already has," said Pandus. "He meant what he said. He's just not cut out for all the responsibilities he has here."

"Yes," said the rabbit: "opening gates, closing gates . . . helping carry linens . . . looking around . . . vans . . ."

"His is a nervous temperament," Pandus continued. "He needs to rest. As for me . . ." — he looked away towards the windows, into the distance beyond — "I do so long to expand my culinary repertoire, to perfect my art . . . to work not just with bananas, but with other things . . . with bamboo shoots above all. I was beginning to despair, to think my dreams of a restaurant of my own would remain forever unrealized. I'd lost hope. It's a terrible day when you lose hope — it makes you a little insane. Then Blue found that book and told me about it, and then came one night of madness when, over carrots and shoots, we hatched this wicked plan." He looked back at Gorilla. "I'm so ashamed, milord, when you've been so good to us. We allowed ourselves to be overwhelmed by our own discontents. It was . . . shameful."

"Shameful," echoed Blue Bunny, though at a higher pitch.

Gorilla looked from one to the other several times and then sighed. He scratched his head. He sighed again. He scratched his head again. "I've been inconsiderate," he said at last in a doleful voice. "I hadn't realized. I was so wrapped up in all my own many grave responsibilities that I hadn't noticed . . ."

Here he paused, however, because Rolandus had suddenly begun coughing very loudly and had turned away with his paws over his mouth.

"I really am concerned about your health, Roly," said Gorilla. "You must look after it. Anyway, as I was saying, I've been so caught up in my duties as Laird that I haven't noticed what tremendous burdens have been laid on your poor shoulders. I'm sorry. It's all my fault and I think it's time I put matters right. Pandus," — he looked at the chef frankly — "stealing is wrong, you know, but so is wasting one's talents. Just this morning my friends were telling me I'm rich. I am, Roly, aren't I?"

"Immensely, sir," said the dog, fighting down a final cough.

"Well, there you have it. I could just give you the money to set up in business. I think it would be jolly. All I ask is that you train a replacement chef, and share your recipes so we don't have to do without all your marvelous dishes, and . . . Oh, I know!" He clapped his hands together three times ecstatically. "You can train me! I can be the replacement chef!"

Rolandus cleared his throat loudly. "Ah, sir, I think you're forgetting . . . ah, forgetting your own many . . . your own very grave responsibilities. You know, the rubber balls, and bananas, and . . . other rubber balls . . ."

Gorilla considered this for a moment, pensively tapping his lips with his forefinger. "Yes, that's true. I do see your point. Good old Roly, always bringing me back to earth. But who could we . . . ?"

"Perhaps Panda," Rolandus said. "She's already quite proficient in the kitchen, and already knows many of chef's recipes inside and out."

Panda, who had been sitting quietly with downcast eyes, now looked up in surprise at Gorilla, who was already smiling back at her.

"I say, Panda old girl," said Gorilla, "would you like that?"

"Oh, yes, sir," said Panda, almost having to catch her breath. "It's something I've dreamed of doing."

"But, milord," said Pandus softly, "this is all so . . . ridiculously generous of you. Are you sure? I mean, after I tried . . . ?"

"There's no more to be said on the matter," Gorilla interrupted. "Everyone accidentally steals a treasure from a castle now and then. Just so long as one learns a valuable lesson from it, there's nothing to worry about. And restaurants are just so jolly. I shall come once a week, and eat banana custards, and we'll talk about goings-on here at the castle. It will be so nice to get away from all my duties now and then. And, now, Blue — " He turned to the rabbit.

171

"Yes, sir?" said Blue Bunny hopefully, his ears beginning to rise up from his head.

"Since your job is wearing you down so, I've the perfect solution. It's an absolute inspiration."

"Yes, sir?"

"You're fired."

"Oh." Blue Bunny's ears drooped again. "Oh." He folded his hands in his lap. "You mean you're . . . "

"Giving you the sack, yes. That's the phrase, isn't it? I'm setting you free. Isn't that wonderful? Now you can go to your cottage in the hills without worrying about us here. But" — Gorilla paused for a second and rubbed his chin — "won't you be terribly lonely up there all on your own?"

Blue Bunny's lips trembled a bit and a look of torment came into his eyes. "Yes, sir, I will," he said forcefully, "I always knew I would. But, oh sir, what am I to do? I need the rest. I can't . . . cope."

"I know, but . . . " Suddenly Gorilla smiled. "You know, I think we have some cottages around the grounds here. I'm almost sure I've noticed some. Do we, Roly?"

"Yes, sir," said the dog, "a few."

"Well, there we are," said Gorilla with an enormous grin. "That's perfect. We'll put you in one of those, and set up a nice large garden patch for you, and you can live there and grow things. Oh," — he hopped in delight and clapped his hands again — "you can come for visits here at the castle! You'll be right next door! You can come for tea! And I can come visit you, too!"

"Sir," said Blue Bunny, relief and gratitude flooding his features and his voice, "that's so, sir, so very kind, sir, so . . . "

"And I'll bring my bagpipes along! Every day! You can listen to me rehearse. Oh, it'll be so merry!"

Blue Bunny froze. For several seconds, his eyes remained exceedingly wide and his mouth remained fixed in an idiotic grin. "Well, sir," he finally said, his voice surprisingly subdued. "Sir . . . " He swallowed hard and his expression became somewhat more sober. "I don't want you to feel you have to . . . to perform just for . . . "

"No," said Rolandus in a very calm voice, flashing the rabbit a rather steely stare, "I think that's an altogether excellent idea. It couldn't be more fitting. Don't you agree, Blue?"

The rabbit returned the dog's gaze for a moment, clearly searching for something to say. Then, smiling feebly, he nodded. "It will be . . . wonderful, sir. I look forward to it."

"You see, Piggles," said Gorilla, turning to Porculina, "everything worked out just splendidly. Murphy has triumphed again."

Porculina opened her mouth to say something.

Gorilla, however, was borne along by his own good spirits. With a grand sweep of his arms that took in the whole room, he said, "You see, we should all be friends — fluffy friends forever. That's my favorite motto. Well, that and 'one good hand is worth two old bushes any time.' I say, Pandus, what's on for tea?"

Epilogue

SEVERAL MINUTES LATER, AMID A BABBLE OF SMALL conversations, the occupants of the sitting room began to disperse to get ready for their tea. Pandus, again shyly expressing his gratitude to Gorilla, departed with Panda for the kitchens, and Blue Bunny, still quivering with embarrassment and happiness, asked Rolandus if he might go below with them to help.

"Of course," said the dog.

* * *

On her way out, Miss Raccoon paused to talk to Teddy. "You were so brave and clever!" she gushed. "It's always thrilling to see a professional at work, especially one so fearless." And her dark and lovely eyes positively twinkled at him.

Teddy blushed but managed to say, "Thank you" without swallowing too loudly. "I so look forward to your next film," he added.

* * *

As the frogs were departing the room, Jumping Bean complained to his uncle, "I didn't get to help in catching the thieves at all!"

"Aye, weel, true," said Ribbit, laying a hand on his nephew's shoulder, "but catchin' flies is more in our line. Teddy Bears are much better at this sort of thing."

* * *

"I must concur," said Alasdair MacAw to Teddy, having overheard the frogs. "Forgive me if I occasionally seemed a bit irate. Parrots too often stand upon their dignity. Well done, Mr Bear, well done."

"You're very gracious," said Teddy.

"Will you be coming to tea?"

"I wouldn't miss it."

The parrot smiled. "I do hope there's something other than banana dishes," he said.

Gorilla, who was standing nearby talking to Porculina, glanced at the parrot with a slight frown, but then merely shook his head in wonder and smiled.

* * *

As he was swaying towards the door on his fins and tentacles, Cuttles turned aside to talk to Teddy, Gorilla, and Porculina. "I hope you three do not expect this happy ending to be the final word on the matter."

"Oh, I do," said Gorilla.

"Hmmph," said the squid. He shrugged. "Perhaps it will be. Sad. I wanted to capture this mighty tale in verse — in a play. But, I don't know if I can set my tentacle to anything other than tragedy. I've never tried." He then turned a single great golden eye on Teddy. "I understand that you too are something of a literary personage, Mr Bear."

"I'm attempting to be," said Teddy.

"Perhaps we could collaborate," said Cuttles.

"Oh, well," said Teddy, slightly taken aback, "that would of course be a great honor. I mean, to work with so notable an artist. But, um, well, I don't really have all my writing implements and such here with me . . . "

"Not to worry," Gorilla interrupted happily, "I've a whole unopened box of crayons."

"It's settled then," said the squid. "Oh dear, I seem to have sprayed a bit of ink on your fine tie. Well, never mind." He smiled sadly and wobbled away.

* * *

"Ye know," said Woof to the three friends, "family tradition says I shouldna think weel of a privileged aristocrat, but I canna help it. Ye're as fine and

176

generous and goodhearted a soul as I'll ever know, Laird MacGorilla, and ye preside over a grand and goodhearted clan."

"Yes, his heart *is* good and kind and generous," said Porculina warmly.

"And wise," Teddy added.

"I'm so glad you stayed for dinner," said Gorilla. "It wouldn't have been nearly so jolly without you."

"Weel, must wash m' paws before m' tea."

*   *   *

"Miss, sirs," said Rolandus before departing to prepare for tea, "it has been an adventurous two days so far. I hope there'll be no more undue excitement hereafter."

"It's been absolutely thrilling!" said Porculina. "And you were so cool and collected the whole time!"

"Yes, miss," said the dog, "so I was."

"I don't know what I'd do without old Roly," said Gorilla.

"I dread to think, sir," said Rolandus with a polite tilt of the head. "If you will excuse me."

"Thank you," said Teddy.

*   *   *

Ten minutes later, as they were passing through the foyer towards a large drawing room on the far side of the castle where tea was to be served, Teddy, Porculina, and Gorilla paused before the great statue of the Grand Gorilla of Mickle Fame.

"Such a stirring figure," remarked Porculina. "You have such a wonderful family history, Gor-Gor. Mine is so boring by comparison."

Gorilla nodded. "That's true." Then, a moment later, he said, "Teddy, will you take me up on my offer? I mean, to come live here? Oh, please say yes. It would be so delightful. You'd be here, and I'd be here, and Piggles would be just down in London, and she could come visit us, and we could go visit her, and we could all go visit . . . somewhere else and when you went on your daring travel writer trips we might join you . . . "

"I have a cousin in France, too," remarked Teddy.

"Oh, please please please," said Gorilla, rocking back and forth eagerly, "please please please, please please . . . "

"Yes, do," Porculina said suddenly. "It really would be wonderful."

Teddy looked around him, at the vast foyer and the soaring ceiling and the great statue, and then at the faces of his two oldest friends. "I can't think of any place where I'd be happier," he said.

As they were approaching the door of the drawing room a few minutes later, walking through a carpeted corridor with small portraits of the noble MacGorillas of yore all along the walls, Gorilla said, "There's only one disappointing thing about the way all this ended."

"What's that, Gor-Gor?" asked Porculina.

"I was so hoping we would get to see Henry," he said, "and we didn't."

"Yes," said Teddy, "that's very true."

And, with that, the three friends went in to have their tea.

The End

At the time of this book's writing, DAVID BENTLEY HART was 45 years old and PATRICK ROBERT HART was 11. One of the two authors is the other's father and one is the other's son, but you must guess which is which. Both are older now. One has grown wiser, the other has gone bald.

JEROME ATHERHOLT is a graduate of the Schuler School of Fine Art in Baltimore, MD where he also taught for 11 years. For the last 23 years he has been a senior artist at FIRAXIS Games in Maryland and lives with his family in Pennsylvania.

Printed in Great Britain
by Amazon

38730417R00108